Susan Glick

one SHOT

Henry Holt and Company

New York

With love and thanks to my husband, Bruce,
and my children, Aaron, Renee, and David,
for their unwavering support

Henry Holt and Company, LLC
Publishers since 1866
115 West 18th Street
New York, New York 10011
www.henryholt.com

Henry Holt is a registered trademark of
Henry Holt and Company, LLC
Copyright © 2003 by Susan Glick
Distributed in Canada by H. B. Fenn and Company Ltd.

Library of Congress Cataloging-in-Publication Data
Glick, Susan.
One shot / Susan Glick.
p.   cm.
Summary: While living with her newly remarried father in a
Washington, D.C., suburb, fifteen-year-old Lorrie spends the summer working
for and becoming close to an elderly, famous photographer.
[1. Photography—Fiction. 2. Old age—Fiction.
3. Interpersonal relations—Fiction.] I. Title.
PZ7.G4884 On 2003   [Fic]—dc21   2002067887

ISBN 0-8050-6844-9
First Edition—2003
Printed in the United States of America on acid-free paper. ∞
1   3   5   7   9   10   8   6   4   2

This is for Mary

one

Lorrie's dad was sitting on the end of the diving board, his toes tapping the surface of the water. "This is going to be a big year for you," he said, panting slightly. He'd just swum a hundred laps or something.

Lorrie, stretched out in the water beneath him, didn't know how he kept track. She'd lose count around seven, so she just watched the big clock her stepmom had hung on the back wall of the house. She was up to twenty-seven minutes. Pretty good, considering that on Thursday, her first night here, she'd only been able to swim fourteen minutes before giving up.

"This program at Whitman is a wonderful opportunity," he went on, his voice carrying across the water. "A real chance to prove yourself."

Lorrie was sick of hearing about Whitman. Right now she was more interested in seeing how long she could float. Arching her back, she kicked her feet up to the surface. Her ears were under, and her dad's voice was muffled. She didn't need to hear every word. She knew already that he was *so* glad she was here, he was *so* sure she would like Maryland's schools better than those in that little rural town in Pennsylvania where she'd been with her mom for the last two years, and he was *so* happy Lorrie was getting to know his new wife, Elaine.

Lorrie's feet were sinking. She filled her lungs with air and lifted her lower body back up to the surface. Normally she would have listened more carefully to her dad. He didn't usually lecture, but she'd heard all this before. Yesterday, in fact, when she'd taken the subway into the city to meet him for lunch at the Smithsonian National Museum of American History. Her dad was curator of special exhibits. He liked her to come to "D.C.," as they often referred to the nation's capital, and see the new displays and meet the "young folks" on his staff.

Suddenly she realized it was quiet. She lifted her head out of the water, and her legs sank. Her dad was looking at her, waiting. Treading water now, she replayed the last sounds she'd heard. Had he asked a question? "Uh, what was that, Dad?"

"I said, aren't you happy that you and Sarah have stayed in touch? She can show you around, maybe introduce you to the kids on the school paper."

"That'll be great." Sarah and Lorrie had grown up together. Lorrie had lived a couple of blocks from here before her parents divorced. She and Sarah liked to think of themselves as cousins, even though it wasn't true. Their families shared a distant connection by marriage, not blood, but it was a link that had fascinated them as children.

Lorrie looked at her dad through long wet strands of brown hair that stuck to her forehead and hung down across her eyes. She ducked and came up with her head thrown back. There was no way she was going to hassle with this heavy wet hair all summer—not with a pool right here in the backyard that she could jump into anytime she wanted. She made up her mind to cut it, maybe even later today.

Her dad was tossing around all the buzz words now. Gifted and Talented. Accelerated Learner. Advanced Placement. Lorrie hated this. At her old school, she was just your typical "good student," the kind who listened in class and did all the homework, played some sports, worked on the school newspaper. She got good grades. Big deal. So did a lot of kids.

Lorrie did somersaults underwater. This was something she and Sarah used to do when they were little and spent whole summers at the neighborhood pool, over on Fernwood Road. They'd stay in the water all day, playing Marco Polo and seeing how many lengths of the pool they could swim without coming up for air.

With ease, Lorrie did five somersaults in a row. It was something you didn't forget, she figured, like riding a bike.

Now her dad was talking about some big school project that was due on the third day back. Summer reading. Lorrie piled her wet hair on top of her head. She'd have to get the list from Sarah.

Having finally exhausted the subject of Lorrie's "academic career," as he liked to call it, her dad did a neat pike dive and swam to the ladder at the shallow end of the pool. Lorrie joined him on the flagstone deck.

If he'd noticed her indifference to the thrilling topic of Walt Whitman High School, he didn't show it. "I'm glad you're here," he said happily, encircling her with his arm and kissing her wet cheek. He threw his towel over his shoulders. "Oh, I almost forgot. Elaine wants to speak with you when she gets home. You'll be around for the next hour or so, won't you?"

"I'll be sitting right here, drying off," Lorrie said, rubbing sunblock onto her arms. The June sun was hot, and she had burned a little yesterday. She wondered what her new stepmom could want.

Stepmom. She was still getting used to the word. Her dad had remarried in January, after having been separated from Lorrie's mom for three years. Last fall, before the wedding, he'd said, "Maybe you two could be friends." That's probably what all divorced parents said when they remarried, but, of course, the whole idea was silly. Elaine was forty or something. Lorrie wasn't looking for a friend her mom's age. And she wasn't looking for another mom, either. She was going to be sixteen this fall. She was almost through with mothers.

Lorrie was on the verge of sleep when Elaine came out an hour or so later. She was wearing a pale pink suit, a dressy outfit for a Saturday morning at the office, Lorrie thought. In each hand, she held a can of Orange Crush. A bag of pretzels was tucked under her arm.

"Sorry, I didn't mean to wake you," she said when Lorrie lifted her head and rolled over on her back. Lorrie reached for the soda Elaine was offering. "I'm up."

Spreading a towel over the chair next to Lorrie's, Elaine stretched out, leaning back contentedly and surveying the pool. "I've got to get in there and scrub that grout," she said, making it sound as though she was looking forward to it. Lorrie knew that Elaine loved her pool. She'd had it put in this March, and she'd been swimming in it since the end of April.

"So, Lorrie, did Roger mention to you that I'm quitting my job?" Elaine asked, getting right to the point.

"No," Lorrie blurted out, her Orange Crush dripping

over her bottom lip. Her dad hadn't said a thing about it! How could he have gone on and on about high school when *this* was happening?

Elaine was one of those workaholics you hear about, the kind of person who puts in a million hours a week at her law firm downtown. "This is a joke, right?" asked Lorrie.

Elaine was studying the pool tile, thinking about grout, no doubt. "Your dad couldn't believe it, either." She chuckled softly, slipping out of her silk jacket. Her hair was back in a gold clasp that she pulled out now. Giving her head a shake, she lifted her face into the early-summer sun.

"My dad's big on commitments," Lorrie offered, still stunned by the news.

Elaine laughed easily, the sound bouncing off the surface of the water and filling the backyard.

"He is," Lorrie insisted. "He just hates it when we quit things—" Uh-oh. Lorrie hadn't meant to say "we." It was a reflex—a dumb one, too, since her parents had been apart for years. She started over. "I mean, my dad has a thing about people—me—starting something and not finishing it."

Elaine looked interested.

Lorrie closed her mouth. This conversation wasn't about her, and it most definitely wasn't going to be about her mother. It was just that her mom had driven her dad crazy, dropping things she'd started. It wasn't little stuff, either, like sewing projects or refinishing furniture. It was big stuff, like apartment leases and new jobs.

Elaine munched on a pretzel and looked thoughtful. "What did you ever start and not finish?"

That was an easy one. "In middle school, I wanted to play the flute. I joined the school band, but I really hated it. Right from the start. I didn't like the way it felt against my mouth, and I never practiced."

"So you quit?"

"I tried. My dad talked me into finishing out the year." She carefully ate the salt off her pretzel. That wasn't quite the truth. Her dad had encouraged her not to drop the flute but had left it up to her, since she was the one who had to practice every day. She'd planned to quit, but then she just couldn't do it. So she started up again with her practicing, working extra hard until she got caught up. But for now, she shrugged. "He hates quitters."

"Well, I'm not a quitter," Elaine said, sounding amused.

Lorrie popped the pretzel into her mouth.

"I've been at this firm since I got out of law school. Eighteen years of sixty-hour workweeks. That's a whole lot of billable hours."

Lorrie thought about this. "Eighteen years," she said. "You've been there my whole life and then some."

Elaine groaned. "When you put it like that, it sounds even worse. Well, I've got just a little bit longer." Ever since she sat down, she'd been discarding her work clothes. Her jacket, her hair clip, her shoes. Now she pulled out her earrings. "I need to change into my bathing suit," she said, standing up. "Can you hold on a minute? There's something I want to discuss with you."

What else could there be? Lorrie wondered as Elaine disappeared into the changing room. Then it occurred to Lorrie that Elaine hadn't mentioned another job.

Oh, no, thought Lorrie, shaking her damp head. She was *not* going to spend the summer with her stepmother. That was just not part of the deal. The deal had been for her to come here, rather than go with her mom to California, so that she could spend the summer hanging out with Sarah, sitting by the pool, taking bike rides, going downtown to shop in Georgetown, and working a couple of days a week at a part-time job that she planned on finding this week. She already had an interview on Monday with a woman down the street who did day care in her home.

Before Lorrie could feel any sorrier for herself, Elaine was back, dressed now in a black Speedo with a splash of colors across the front. She, like Lorrie's dad, was an exercise fanatic. Sometimes they ran together in the early mornings. They were talking about running the Marine Corps Marathon this fall.

Taking a seat crossways on the chaise longue, Lorrie's stepmom got right down to business. "Okay, here's the thing," she said. "I'd like to offer you a job for the summer. Maybe part-time into the fall as well. We'll have to see how it goes."

"I don't get it."

"Of course not. I'm sorry. Let me begin again. I'll be starting a new job next week—very part-time to start—and I'll need an assistant. I'm doing some work for a woman named Molly Price. Have you heard of her?"

Lorrie shook her head.

"She's a photographer. Quite famous, in fact. Or used to be, anyway, when she was younger. She's in her eighties now."

Lorrie knew some contemporary women photographers whose work she liked, women like Annie Leibovitz, Mary Ellen Mark, and Carol Guzy.

"She lives a few blocks from here, over on Roosevelt Street," Elaine went on.

"Near my old house."

"Right. Very near to where you used to live with your parents," Elaine said, adding this detail easily. "Anyway, Molly needs some help settling her estate."

"Oh, so you'd be her lawyer?"

"Yes, and more. You see, Molly's been in that house for the past forty years and, for the last decade anyway, she's been—well—I guess the best way to put it is to say she's been a hermit. She's closed herself off from the world."

Lorrie frowned. "And *what* is it you're going to do?"

"She has a lifetime of work crammed into that house. Boxes of photos and negatives, as well as her own private collections of the work of other famous photographers who were her friends. And she's got letters—file cabinets full of correspondence that she's held on to all these years." Elaine looked at Lorrie. "She needs someone to go through it with her and help her make decisions. There's a fair amount of paperwork, legal paperwork, involved."

"Sounds like a big job."

"It is. Everyone wants to own her collections. Museum curators from all over the world have been requesting access for years, but she refuses everyone. Biographers, historians, art galleries, colleges." Elaine shook her head. "No, this isn't just some old lady with a house full of junk."

"So what's her problem? If everyone wants it, why doesn't she just give it to them?"

"She's hard to figure out."

"But she talks to you?"

"Yes, that's the strange part. We struck up a friendship several summers ago, when I lived over on Jefferson. I'd see her in the garden out front, and I'd stop and chat. Sometimes I'd pull a weed or two. I didn't know who she was, so I guess she felt comfortable with me. In the winter sometimes I'd check on her if I hadn't seen her in a while. And over the years I've helped her hire people to mow the lawn and fix the roof—that sort of thing. She doesn't usually open the door to people who come knocking, but she lets me in and serves me tea, too." Elaine sounded proud of the fact.

Lorrie was curious about this woman, once so famous and now such a recluse.

"I'll be needing someone to help me. And I thought of you. Are you interested?" Elaine asked.

"Interested?"

"Yes. I'll be assisting Molly with legal decisions—she's setting up grants and scholarships, too—but I'll need help with the other tasks, sorting through papers, moving around boxes, possibly getting the house ready to sell. Mundane, hands-on work."

"Wait. She's moving?"

"She's considering an assisted-care apartment. She hasn't made up her mind, though her name is on the waiting list. They have a doctor on staff, and they provide meals and social activities." Elaine chuckled. "For some reason, I just can't imagine Molly playing bingo."

"Is she sick or something?"

"No, not at all. Well, I guess I shouldn't say that. She has medicine for her heart, for low blood pressure, I believe, but she's still pretty feisty," Elaine said, smiling. "I'd love it if you'd work with me." Her voice was warm. "I'll pay you a couple of bucks above minimum wage to start. Later in the summer, if Molly does decide to move out and we get to painting the rooms, we'll go a little higher." She stood up and did some stretching exercises that looked like yoga. Lorrie knew she was getting ready to swim laps. Elaine didn't time herself or her laps, like Lorrie and her dad. She just swam.

Lorrie needed time to think. She wanted to work this summer so she could save for a car, but working with her stepmother at some old lady's house was definitely not what she had in mind, though the thought of meeting this famous photographer was kind of intriguing.

Elaine dipped a foot in the pool and splashed water onto the sunny deck, darkening the blue stone. "Think about it. I don't need an answer right this minute," she said, shielding her eyes from the sun when she looked back at Lorrie. "Why don't you come with me on Monday? I'm going over in the morning to do some preliminary work. You can meet her, maybe help me get started. And then decide."

"Just meet her?"

"Yeah. It'll be quick. Maybe an hour. I need to go over some papers with her. You can come along and get to know her a little bit. I should warn you, she's kind of abrasive sometimes."

"Abrasive?"

Elaine knelt down and swished the water up over her shoulders.

"I think you'll like her. I know you'll love her work."

Lorrie considered this for a moment. She was interested, that was for sure. And not just because Molly was famous. It was the photography. Lorrie's work on the school paper had been the best part of her sophomore year. Especially when one of her photos was reprinted in the town paper, the *Clearfield News*.

"Okay, I'll come along," she agreed.

"That's great," said Elaine happily. "Just don't let her get to you and you'll be fine."

"What does *that* mean?"

Elaine slid into the pool. "Molly is hard to describe," she said, plucking a leaf from the water. "You'll just have to see for yourself."

Lorrie waited for Elaine to say more, but her stepmom began to swim. What was it about this old lady that Elaine wasn't telling her?

two

It was the strangest feeling, having all her hair gone. Lorrie couldn't keep her hands off the top of her head. She knew that her hair had been heavy when it was wet, but she'd never realized that even dry hair weighed so much.

Yesterday, by the time she'd ridden her bike into downtown Bethesda, it was almost five. Near closing time on Saturday. The woman at the shop didn't look too happy to see her. Lorrie grabbed a magazine and showed her a short, layered cut. "Like this," she had directed. "Short. Edgy. You know, like something you might see in New York."

"Big change," the woman noted, pinning up the first piece of Lorrie's long, fine hair. It *was* a big change, Lorrie realized the next morning as she sat by the pool, anticipating her dad and Elaine's return home from the early church service they went to on Sundays. If she'd been with her mom, this wouldn't have mattered, but her father hated surprises. She didn't know what Elaine might say.

It was a gorgeous morning, not too hot yet. She knew they'd come look for her by the pool, so she stretched out on the floating chaise and tried to read her book.

Her dad came through the sliding door first. "What the—" he sputtered, and stopped so abruptly that his coffee splashed down the front of the newspaper he was carrying. Lorrie's hand instinctively went to the top of her head, where it'd spent a good bit of time already this morning.

"What did you *do?*" he gasped, coming closer.

"I cut it. I mean, I had it cut. Yesterday. After you guys went out. I'd been thinking about it for a while. It gets in my way when I'm taking pictures. And now, with the pool . . ." She shrugged. "So yesterday I just did it." She wished her dad would stop looking so stunned.

His frown deepened.

Lorrie gave her head a toss and addressed both her father and Elaine, who had just joined her dad on the deck. "So—you haven't said whether you like it," she said, trying to sound sure of herself.

Elaine nodded her head approvingly, but Lorrie's dad didn't look happy at all. "Don't you think you should have gotten permission?" he demanded.

"Permission? Permission to cut my hair?" Lorrie almost laughed. "It's just a haircut, Dad. It's not like I got a tattoo or a nose ring or something."

There was a long moment of silence between them, and Lorrie could see that her father was thinking this through, wondering if he should exert more authority. "Sorry, Dad," she said lightly. "Next time I'll let you know in advance. I promise. I know you hate surprises."

Elaine sent Lorrie's father a smile. "Oh, Roger, it's beautiful." Setting her coffee cup down on the table by her chair, she came closer to Lorrie. "I love it. Has Sarah seen it yet?"

Lorrie shook her head and kept shaking it, feeling the lightness of having her hair gone. "She called last night from her grandmother's in Chicago. She's not coming in until late tomorrow."

At last, the frown was gone from her dad's face. "Lorrie, it looks very nice."

"Thanks, Dad." She cocked her head, teasing him now. "I was going to color it while I was at it, a very pretty orange or green, but the shop was closing." She leaned back in her drifting chair. "I guess I'll just have to live with this mousy brown for a while."

"Mousy brown?" her father protested, touching his own hair, which was the same color. "It's a rich, dark chestnut."

Lorrie laughed and didn't mention that half of her dad's hair was already gray.

"You can always try lemon juice," suggested Elaine.

"Don't encourage her," said Lorrie's dad.

"Yeah, Elaine, don't encourage me. I don't want to do anything too *radical.*"

Elaine got in the water. "That's the word my partners used when I told them I was quitting," she muttered.

Lorrie saw the look that her dad gave Elaine, but she didn't know what it meant. Had it been her real mother, a big argument would have begun that would have lasted for the next hour or, more likely, for the rest of the day. But now the moment quietly passed, and the two adults went on to discuss what bush to plant by the backyard gate.

....

The next morning, Lorrie stood in front of her closet, examining her clothes. It wasn't like this first visit with Molly was a job interview, but it felt like it.

She had no idea what to wear, though she could make a pretty good guess that she didn't have it. By the end of this past school year, all her clothes were too small or had worn out, but she hadn't wanted to buy anything until she got here and could shop with Sarah. Bethesda was an upscale suburb of Washington, full of lawyers and doctors and people who worked for the federal government. It was nothing like the little Pennsylvania town she'd just moved away from. Kids dressed differently here.

In the end, she chose one of her newer pairs of jeans and a T-shirt without any writing on it. It wasn't what she'd wear to a real interview, but hopefully it was presentable enough. When she went downstairs, she was relieved to see that Elaine was wearing a similar outfit.

On the way over, neither of them spoke much. Once Elaine pointed to a house with paint colors she liked. Another time she said, "I ran over a squirrel here last week." Lorrie was beginning to feel pretty comfortable with her new stepmom. She wasn't one of those adults who asked you a million questions while they were trying to get to know you.

Molly's house was a big two-story colonial, white with black shutters. The paint was peeling, and one of the upstairs shutters was hanging a little crooked. The lawn was mowed and trimmed, but the small garden plot by the street was high with weeds.

"This isn't like her," Elaine said, yanking out a tall piece of grass on her way to the front door. "She's been letting the backyard go for years, but never this little garden."

Elaine lifted the heavy knocker and let it drop. Lorrie watched a piece of red paint fall to the doormat. They waited and listened, and Elaine knocked again. Inside, the house was quiet.

Suddenly the door swung open. "You could have come on in," the little old lady barked. "You needn't have made me come all the way to the front door to answer it."

"Good morning, Molly," Elaine said. If she was disturbed by Molly's greeting, she didn't let on. "If you don't want to come to the door, you'll have to give me a key." Then she turned to Lorrie, who'd taken a step or two backward at the sound of Molly's voice. "I brought my husband's daughter with me. Lora. Lorrie Taylor, Molly Price."

Elaine seemed to be waiting for the two of them to do something, so Lorrie tentatively put forth her hand. "I'm glad to meet you, Ms. Price."

The old woman took her hand but glared at her. "Molly. It's Molly. No one calls me Ms. anything. Now, come on in. I've got on that blooming air-conditioning, and we're letting in the hot, humid air."

Lorrie generally liked older people, but she wasn't too sure about this lady. Molly seemed cranky and mean. Behind Molly's back, Elaine gave Lorrie what was supposed to be an encouraging grin, but Lorrie just shook her head in disgust.

Though Molly's tongue was fast, her body wasn't. She moved with excruciating slowness, taking one careful step at a time. With one hand, she steadied herself on the furniture or the doorjambs. With her other hand, she clasped together the two sides of an old green sweater as if a fierce wind were going to blow it off her thin shoulders.

"And don't think I'm going to keep this house as cool as you might like, either. I don't like those cold drafts on my feet."

But as they walked slowly through the hall, Lorrie forgot about Molly. Lorrie loved old buildings like this one. This house, with its high ceilings and wide molding along the top and bottom of the walls, was much older than the one she lived in. The wavy glass in the windows told her that it had been here way before the other houses in the neighborhood. Probably one of the original homesteads, she figured, thinking like her father, the historian.

Molly and Elaine at her side were progressing so slowly that Lorrie felt free to remain behind and continue poking her head into the open doorways of the first-floor rooms. The house must have been beautiful, she decided, glancing up to admire the wide landing of the turning staircase that looked like something out of a movie. But it had been neglected over the years. The wallpaper was lifting up in places, and the paint on the ceiling of the dining room off to the right was peeling in sheets. It had been years since someone had been in here with a paintbrush.

Then Lorrie saw the first photograph. She looked around the rooms. Pictures were everywhere. Above the sofa, across the mantelpiece, along the top of the dining-room sideboard.

Lorrie had told Elaine and Sarah that she wasn't familiar with Molly's work, but that wasn't true. The black-and-white photo in front of her was in her history book from last semester, when they'd studied the migrant farm workers in California. Lorrie would never forget the desperate look in that mother's eyes as she stared into the camera, her barefoot children beside her. And next to it, above the sofa, hung a famous shot of Dr. Martin Luther King, Jr., speaking to a huge crowd on the mall downtown in the 1960s. She'd seen that picture a hundred times, but not the one beside it, a more intimate shot of King, where he stood alone in a moment of quiet prayer in a church. She supposed it was rude to leave Molly and snoop around like this, but she couldn't help herself. The pictures held her spellbound.

She was moving toward the sounds of Elaine and Molly talking, when a grouping of color photos at the foot of the staircase stopped her again. There were five in all, pictures from a jungle. Since the photos were in color, Lorrie figured it was Vietnam.

The soldier in the picture—in all the pictures—was young, probably twenty or so. In the first shot, he was grinning broadly, flirting with the camera. He had a football tucked under his arm and wore a baseball cap back on his head, projecting that boy-next-door look. Lorrie half-smiled at the picture, responding naturally to his charm.

Her smile quickly faded. In the subsequent shots, the baseball cap was replaced by a helmet and the football by a big ugly gun. Gone, too, was the charming grin, and in its place, a chilling expression of fear that he wore until the final photo, when the gun had fallen from his hands and his lips had returned to a smile, a sad one this time, at the moment of his death.

Lorrie found herself going through the sequence of shots again and again, each time looking for more and then finding it. The cigarette tucked playfully behind his ear in the first shot, the grenades tucked into his belt in the second, the dirt on his face as he crouched in the ditch, the dark splotch of blood on his leg, and, finally, the trickle of sweat on his lip above his death-smile in the final frame.

Lorrie was still standing there, wishing she could shoot like this, when she heard Elaine calling her name.

"Then there's the Library of Congress," Elaine was saying as Lorrie entered the sunny kitchen. "And Natalie Dunn from the University of Maryland College of Journalism. She's very eager to meet you." Elaine had a legal pad in front of her and a calendar. She was pointing to the end of July.

From the kitchen doorway, Lorrie stared at Molly's back, trying to imagine the woman in front of her taking the pictures she'd just seen. She wanted to ask her about the soldier and the migrant worker. She wanted to ask how she'd gotten the shot of Dr. King in church.

"Molly, let's get a few dates on the calendar. How about July twenty-sixth?" Elaine asked, all business.

Molly put both hands on the table before her and with a great effort pushed herself up and out of her chair. "I'm going to make us some tea," she announced, ignoring Elaine's question completely.

Lorrie's feelings for Molly had softened since she'd seen the photos. She felt a return of that kind of sweet affection that older people usually brought out in her. Patting Molly on the arm, as she would her own grandmother, she said gently, "I'll get it. Just tell me where everything is."

Molly yanked her arm away. "Don't you be babying me like I'm on death's doorstep. I can good and well still make us a pot of tea."

Lorrie jumped back. "I'm sorry," she said, stunned by the forcefulness of Molly's voice. She looked to the kitchen door and was about to leave the room—for good, she figured—when Molly spoke again.

"If you're so fired up and ready to help," she barked, "why don't you take out the cups and saucers? They're in the cabinet over there."

Elaine tried to flash Lorrie an encouraging smile, but Lorrie wasn't buying it. This Molly Price might take great pictures and she might be famous for it, but that didn't give her permission to be so rude. Lorrie didn't know how Elaine was going to stand it, working here with her.

Lorrie took her time arranging the cups and saucers, and then, while the teakettle was bringing the water to a boil, she stepped over to the back door and peeked through the curtain. Elaine was right about the backyard. It was a mess out there. The only sign of human life was a small concrete bench, tucked off to the side behind a big tree, an oak. The grass was high, too high to walk through easily, but Lorrie thought she could detect a narrow, trampled path leading to the bench.

A small photograph hanging next to the back door caught Lorrie's eye. It was an older man, white-haired and quite handsome. At his side he held a wide floppy hat, the kind that gardeners wear on a sunny day. With a start, Lorrie realized he was standing by the bench in Molly's backyard. She took a closer look, trying to identify other familiar things in the photo, but nothing looked the same.

The teakettle whistled. As much as she feared Molly's lashing out at her, Lorrie couldn't let her pick up that heavy kettle of boiling water. "I'll get that," she said firmly, and, reaching the stove first, grabbed the steaming kettle and filled the china teapot.

••••••••••••••••••••••

Walking home later, Elaine draped her arm over Lorrie's shoulders and gave her a hug. "She's a character, isn't she?"

Lorrie snorted. "That's one way to put it."

Elaine laughed. "She's got an artistic temperament."

"Remind me never to be an artist." But Lorrie only half-meant it. She'd have given anything to be able to take pictures like Molly Price.

three

By the time she and Elaine reached their street, Lorrie knew she'd take the job. It was the only way she'd get to ask Molly all the questions she wanted answers to. But she had the day ahead of her, and Sarah was still gone, so she decided she'd ride into Bethesda and at least look around at other places where she might work. There were Help Wanted signs everywhere.

She didn't want to work with food, she knew that, so the town's million restaurants were out. There was a big bookstore, and the video store, and a couple of small gift shops that might be okay. She filled out applications and talked to some managers, but nothing sounded as intriguing as working with Molly Price. Lorrie couldn't get those pictures out of her head.

At two o'clock, she went for her interview with the daycare lady on her street and was persuaded to stay and work for the rest of the afternoon. The pay was good, and the woman had offered her an easy, flexible schedule, but after four hours at the job, Lorrie couldn't wait to get out of there. She liked children okay, but these were babies. Little ones in diapers with runny noses, and tempers, too. She never knew babies could be so angry when they didn't get what they wanted.

When she got home, she felt too grungy even to jump in the pool. She took a long shower, threw her clothes into the wash, and was asleep on her bed when her dad called her for dinner.

That evening, Elaine came into her room with her clipboard and legal pad in hand.

"How was the job search?" she asked.

"Did my dad tell you about the babysitting?"

Elaine smiled. "So Molly's is sounding better?"

"Yes, I think so."

"I was hoping you'd say that." Elaine handed Lorrie the yellow pad. "Here are the figures I've come up with," she said, sounding like the lawyer she was. "Don't hold me to the penny, but I think this is what you can count on earning before school starts."

Lorrie stared at the sum at the bottom of the yellow sheet. It looked good.

"I know you're saving for a car," Elaine added.

Lorrie read over the schedule that her stepmom had worked out. Beginning later this week and for the next three weeks or so, until Elaine had finished at the law firm, Lorrie would work half-days. After that, it would be full-time. She and Sarah had planned a whole summer of lounging by the pool, but Sarah had told her on the phone the other night that she'd picked up more hours at the stables. So Lorrie might as well work, too.

"I think this is fine," she agreed.

Elaine clapped her hands, surprising Lorrie with her

enthusiasm. "I'm so glad. Now, let's get one thing straight from the start. Neither of us has done this sort of work before, so let's just agree that if this doesn't work out, for any reason, we'll talk it over and make the necessary changes."

Lorrie wasn't sure she understood.

"What I'm saying is that you're not signing a contract here. If you don't like it, or if you're really not getting along with either Molly or me, you can quit."

"Quit?" Lorrie repeated.

Elaine smiled broadly. "Okay, re-evaluate. We'll re-evaluate whether this is working. How's that?"

Lorrie returned the smile. "That sounds good."

....

Sarah's home! That was the first thing that came into Lorrie's head when she woke up the next morning. Sarah was back, and Lorrie wanted to see her. And she couldn't wait until that night, when Sarah was coming over for dinner. Lorrie decided to ride over and see if she could catch her at the stables. A quick visit, just so that she could tell her friend to bring stuff to sleep over.

The stables were an easy fifteen-minute ride through the neighborhood and onto the bike trail in Rock Creek Park. Lorrie missed the long rides on the hilly roads outside of Clearfield, but the bike path was a pretty nice city trail.

She smelled the barns before she saw them. The scent of horses and manure instantly brought back all her fears. She was afraid of horses, had been for years, ever since she fell that time when she was ten. She straddled her bike near the edge of the parking lot and considered turning around, or, better yet, taking the path down into the city. But that seemed silly. Maybe Sarah was in the office, right inside the door.

Lorrie locked her bike and timidly stepped into the shady barn. The front office was empty. So was the big riding ring. She took a few cautious steps forward. The horses were in stalls back behind the ring's walls. She could hear them snorting and shifting. She cocked her head and listened for the sound of Sarah's voice. There, down at the end of the barn, she could hear someone pitching hay.

Lorrie hesitated. Right now she was standing in a comfortable spot. The entire ring was in front of her. The door was at her back. But to see who was tossing hay, she would have to enter the corridor where the horses were lined up. She took a few tentative steps in that direction. The corridor was dimmer than the ring and front room, though not so dark that she couldn't see the enormous rear ends and tails of the horses standing there. The sound of the pitchfork hitting the concrete floor of the stalls carried easily across the barn.

Lorrie had decided to leave when a quick flash of blue jeans caught her eye. "Sarah?" she called.

The blue-jeaned leg and then the body that was attached to it emerged. It was a guy.

"Hello," he yelled, smiling in greeting. He was wearing a white T-shirt and had hay down the front of him and in his hair, too. He was cute. Sarah hadn't mentioned any young guys working here, just an older couple, Shane and Frances, who was probably that woman Lorrie had seen in the back pen when she'd ridden up. He gestured for her to approach.

"No thanks," Lorrie mumbled, shaking her head. The horses between them might as well have been crocodiles.

As friendly as the boy seemed, and as much as she wanted to ask him about Sarah, Lorrie wasn't about to walk down the corridor.

She wished she'd never come, but it was too late now. He tossed down his pitchfork and was heading toward her.

"Hi," he said again when he reached her. He swept a hand through his sun-bleached hair, and pieces of hay fell to the barn floor. Behind him, the sun shone through a crack between the barn's boards, lighting the hay dust in the air. He was older than she'd thought, probably in college. First year maybe, but home for the summer break.

Finally, she found her voice. "I'm looking for Sarah," she said, realizing only then that she could have just shouted this in the first place. "Sarah O'Connell," she went on. "Is she around?"

He had a nice smile. "She's out on the trail with a group. She should be back soon." He didn't look at his watch.

Lorrie turned to go.

"Wait. Do you want to schedule a lesson?"

"No," Lorrie said, more firmly than she'd intended. "I'm a friend of hers. She's my cousin. I'm home for the summer. Well, for the whole year. My mother just moved out to California, and my father thinks the schools here . . ." Realizing that she was babbling, she deliberately shut her mouth. What was wrong with her? He'd only asked her if she wanted a lesson, and here she was telling him her life story. And that part about Sarah being her cousin. It seemed silly now that they were both in high school.

She felt her cheeks grow warm. It was hot in this barn.

He was looking at her with amusement. "So you're Lorrie. She told me you were coming. Lorrie Taylor from Pennsylvania. I'm Thomas. I'm a friend of Sarah's, too."

Before Lorrie could respond, the horse nearest to them

stepped out of its stall. Without thinking, Lorrie threw herself back against the wooden planks of the wall, letting out a small scream.

Quickly Thomas grabbed the reins and brought the horse up close beside him. "Whoa there, Buttercup," he said, patting the horse on the neck and leading it back into its stall, where he secured the reins.

When he turned around again, he laughed.

Lorrie was mashed up against the barn wall, her fingertips digging into the wood. Seeing that the horse was secure, she let go, falling forward slightly. "I'm a little jumpy around horses," she admitted sheepishly.

"Well, then, you can't possibly be related to Sarah," he said, stepping over and extending his hand. "As I was saying before Buttercup interrupted us, my name's Thomas West. I'm very glad to meet you."

His hand was cool and dry. "Nice to meet you, too," she said, certain now that he was older. No high-school guy would introduce himself with a handshake.

"Sarah won't be long," he said. "Why don't you wait with me?" He tossed his head in the direction from which he'd come.

Lorrie took one look at the long swishing tails of the horses in their stalls. "I think I'll just meet her back at home. She's coming over in a few hours, and I wanted to surprise her."

He kept his glance on her so easily that he was starting to make her more nervous than the horses did. Again, she couldn't help comparing him with the boys she knew. The guys in school never looked at her like this, straight on. And they were always so fidgety, looking down at the ground, pulling stuff out of their pockets, joking with their friends, while they were trying to carry on a so-called conversation. But this time it was she who was babbling and being fidgety and acting like a kid.

Thomas didn't seem to notice. "You can't just leave, Lorrie," he said, saying her name easily. "You know Sarah. She'll let you have it if she finds out you were here and didn't wait. Come on," he said, surprising her by touching her shoulder and pushing her gently ahead and then stepping to her side to keep himself between her and the horses.

Before she could protest, she was moving along. At her side, Thomas kept chatting, telling her a little bit about each horse. And then she was safely down at the other end, where, she was happy to see, there was a door to the pens at the back of the barn. *That's where I'll go if I need to get out of here,* she decided, planning her escape the way her father had taught her to do in a movie theater in case there was a fire.

Thomas left the pitchfork where he'd dropped it and picked up a grooming brush instead. Facing her, he started working on the horse in the nearest stall. Lorrie positioned herself in the doorway and tried to look relaxed—which was tough to do with this friendly, good-looking guy that Sarah hadn't even mentioned and these snorting and shifting horses all over the place. She looked out the doorway. There were two or three kids on horseback, but no sign of Sarah.

"So—you live here now?" Thomas asked, his long arm reaching to the top of the horse's back.

"Yeah, with my dad. And my stepmother, Elaine."

"Your parents are divorced?"

Lorrie nodded. "It's been a couple of years." It wasn't that big a deal anymore. The hard part had been missing her dad so much when she and her mom moved away.

"I've been hearing about you for weeks," Thomas said. He kept talking to her with the same easy rhythm that he used when he brushed the horse. After a while, Lorrie realized that she'd taken a few steps away from the door. When Thomas took a seat on a bale of hay, she came over and sat down on the one next to him.

"Your school is my old rival," he said. "I went to BCC, Bethesda Chevy Chase."

"You graduated?"

"Just. University of Maryland in the fall."

She wished briefly—stupidly—that she was older so that he might be interested in her. But that was dumb.

They talked about high school, and then he told her about Maryland, about why he had chosen that college when he'd gotten into so many others.

Thomas stood up. "Can't let the boss catch me taking too long a break."

Lorrie thought that was her cue to leave, but he surprised her by tossing her the brush he'd been turning over and over in his hands as they'd talked. Instinctively she caught it. "Lend me a hand, will you?" he asked, heading toward a gray spotted horse a few stalls up.

"I—" she began, rubbing the bristles against her open palm.

He turned back to look at her and then said, "You really don't like these guys, do you?"

"I got thrown once," she said, as if that explained everything. "When I was in fifth grade."

"Were you hurt?" His blue eyes were serious.

Lorrie shrugged and tried to make her voice seem casual. "No, not really. But it was scary. My foot got caught in the stirrup and I was dragged a little bit." Her voice caught on the word *dragged*. "Something spooked the horse. Sarah thought maybe a snake or something."

"Sarah was there?"

"Yes. She caught up with my horse and stopped it—after I'd fallen free." Lorrie's mouth felt dry. She tried to clear her throat.

"Good thing you weren't hurt."

"Yeah, that's what everyone said." She looked around her. "I can't believe I'm even in here, in this barn."

Thomas came back and took the brush from her hand, gently loosening her tense fingers. She found herself holding her breath when his skin touched hers.

The sounds of horses entering the barn broke into the moment and made them both turn in the direction of the ring. "I hear Sarah," he said. "She'll be glad to see you."

Lorrie turned to go.

"Come back and we'll ride," he called to her.

Lorrie laughed as she lifted her hand in farewell. As much as she'd like to spend more time with Thomas, she was not going to get on any horse.

"Lorrie," Sarah shouted, her voice bouncing off the tin roof of the oval ring. "Lorrie!" Sarah rode over, stopped her horse up short, and swooped down to give Lorrie a hug. "You're here!" she said in surprise.

Sarah's horse seemed to tower above Lorrie's head. Why did Sarah always choose the biggest horse in the stable?

"Outside," said Lorrie, breathlessly. "I'll be waiting outside." She was across the ring and out of the barn before Sarah could respond.

four

That evening, Lorrie wanted to drown this same friend she'd been so glad to see earlier.

"It's just one lesson," Sarah was saying sweetly, loud enough for Lorrie's dad and Elaine to hear from where they were standing in front of the grill, barbecuing spareribs. "Thomas is concerned—*very* concerned—that you never got back up on that horse after you were thrown."

Lorrie glared at her friend and was about to dunk her when Sarah darted underwater and came up across the pool. Her curly hair looked almost orange when it was wet. "Roger," she began, calling him by his first name as they'd always done between families, "what do you think? My manager offered to give Lorrie a free riding lesson."

"Manager! He's your boss?" Lorrie cried.

"Yes, didn't he tell you?"

No, he hadn't told her. She'd thought he was an employee like Sarah, there to give riding lessons and clean out the stalls.

Lorrie's dad gestured toward Sarah with the two-pronged barbecuing fork. "I've been trying for years to get Lorrie back into riding," he said earnestly. "I hated to see her give up something she loved so much."

"I didn't love it, not like Sarah does," Lorrie protested. "Besides, in Clearfield, people didn't ride for fun like they do here." It was true. No one she went to school with boarded horses, though there were a couple of kids in 4-H. Here it was something rich kids did. At least that's how Lorrie thought of it now that she'd been away for a while and come back.

"You'd love Thomas," Sarah was saying. "He's great with people who are afraid of horses."

"I'm not afraid," Lorrie protested.

Sarah laughed. "Oh, come on."

Lorrie's dad turned to brush the ribs with barbecue sauce. "Why not try it, Lorrie?" he suggested, nonchalantly. "No one is suggesting an entire summer of lessons, but two or three might be enough to put this old fear to rest."

"And he offered to do it for free," added Sarah.

"Pro bono," added Elaine, who hadn't said much during this whole exchange.

Her father would hear none of that. "I would insist on paying him."

Sarah leaned against the side of the pool, so that only Lorrie could see her face. "He won't want to take the money," Sarah said. "Besides," she added, looking right at her friend, "he likes Lorrie."

Lorrie felt her cheeks blush. "I hate you," she mouthed back.

Sarah held her gaze. "I thought this was something you'd be interested in, so I set up a lesson for you next Sunday morning. Thomas is pretty booked, but I thought early morning was okay for you."

"You did *what*?"

"You can cancel if you want. It's no problem if you do. But I don't know why you wouldn't want to spend the morning with a guy as cute as Thomas."

That's when Lorrie lunged, but Sarah swiftly lifted herself out of the water.

By the time Lorrie reached her, Sarah was holding out the serving plate so that Lorrie's father could take the ribs off the grill. She was talking about some history project she'd done last year for school. Lorrie knew the Thomas discussion was over. Once her dad got started on the skirmishes of the Civil War, there was no diverting him.

······················

Sarah had eaten more dinners with the Taylors than Lorrie could count, and they'd been doing sleepovers at each other's houses since third grade, so Sarah was as comfortable at the Taylors' as she was anywhere.

Lorrie's dad loved jazz, but tonight the music he had playing on the pool speakers was classical. Mozart, Lorrie guessed. The four of them sat at the table for hours, eating ribs and corn on the cob and, later, chocolate cake. The conversation drifted easily from topic to topic.

The only thing that made this meal different from the hundreds that had preceded it was the presence of Elaine, but that turned out to be a minor change. Elaine could have a lot to say, but she could also be so quiet that you might forget she was around. Sarah liked her, Lorrie could tell.

At dusk, the bats came out and swooped down for bugs over the pool, and Elaine lit the red citronella candles to keep the mosquitos away from the table.

Somewhere around ten, Lorrie's dad and Elaine excused

themselves and went in for the night. For the first time since Lorrie had moved back here, she and Sarah were alone. They talked about school and friends and this musician Sarah had just met and wanted to get to know better. They picked at what was left of the chocolate cake. The topic came around to Thomas.

"He didn't tell me he was the manager," Lorrie said, feeling too full and content to be angry about anything.

"Yeah, he runs the place. He's good at it, too."

"Hmm." Lorrie didn't want to say too much.

"You aren't still holding out for that guy Barf, are you?"

"Bart," Lorrie corrected. "His name was Bart. And, no, I'm not still holding out for him, as you put it."

"Barf. Bart. Whatever. He sounded like a jerk."

"He was," Lorrie admitted, still disgusted with herself for having had a crush on him for over a year. "Funny how you can't see what losers they are," she said, remembering how stupid she'd felt when she finally figured it out.

"Well, Thomas isn't a jerk," Sarah said simply. "I think he likes you."

"He's older than me."

Sarah shrugged. "Not by much. He turns eighteen this fall. Besides, both of you are smart."

Lorrie smiled. "Like that has anything to do with anything."

"Look, I just thought maybe you two could be friends. I'm not trying to make a big deal out of it."

Lorrie laughed. Sarah made a big deal out of everything. But Lorrie didn't want that to happen this time. Plus, even if she *did* end up taking the lesson, and even if she *did* like Thomas, she didn't want it to be like all the other times when she'd liked a guy and she and Sarah talked about it endlessly.

Lorrie swooped up another glob of icing. "I got a job," she said, licking it off her finger. She watched to see her friend's reaction.

"What? Where?"

Lorrie told Sarah about Molly Price.

Sarah's mouth dropped open. "You are kidding!" she exclaimed. "I don't believe this! We studied her in history class. The immigrant farm workers in California. The Japanese internment camps. She took pictures *everywhere.*"

"Well, she's not everywhere now." Lorrie told Sarah about Molly's being a recluse. "She won't talk to anyone. Just Elaine. And now me, I guess."

"Molly Price. Wow! You are so lucky."

"It's a job, Sarah."

"Right." Sarah was shaking her head. "I'm mucking stalls, and you're talking photography with Molly Price."

"I hope we're talking photography. Right now, we're cleaning house."

"Still," said Sarah.

"Yeah, still," echoed Lorrie. It had the potential for being pretty great.

....

Late that night, after Sarah had fallen asleep on the futon in Lorrie's room, Lorrie got up and went to her desk. Suddenly she was missing her mom.

Her mother was traveling right now, driving her stuff from Pennsylvania to California, and Lorrie wondered, as she sometimes had in the past few days, if she should have gone along with her. At least for the ride out.

But she was angry at her mother, too, angrier than she'd ever been. She hadn't wanted to move. Not in the middle of high school. Clearfield was a small town, not anything like Bethesda, but Lorrie had liked it there. She loved being on the school paper, being the assistant editor in her sophomore year, and taking pictures at all the games. And then there was that photo from the football game when Allan Kyler had made that surprise catch and she'd been right there, just two feet away, for the shot.

She knew she was what they called a big fish in a little pond, but that suited her. Here she wasn't even in a pond. It was an ocean. She was already feeling a little bit lost, even though this was her hometown.

She felt comfortable in Clearfield, where the lady at the drugstore knew her, and the librarian always remembered the last book Lorrie had read. She missed her little house, her room that overlooked a backyard creek, and the bike routes out in the countryside that she'd set up for herself and her two riding buddies from school who would join her.

But her mother, always in search of some new horizon, hadn't settled into the town like Lorrie had. Her mom wanted something different. She wanted to "see the sea" when she woke up in the morning, she'd said—and then expected Lorrie to share that feeling. Without even consulting Lorrie, she'd made up her mind to go, choosing Monterey because of some pictures she'd seen in a magazine.

"She never even asked me," Lorrie had cried to Sarah on the phone the night she knew her mother was serious about California. "She just made the decision as if I were a house pet she could cart along."

Lorrie had been deeply hurt. Even after her mother figured that out and apologized, Lorrie didn't feel like she could forgive her. Sarah told her it would take time—but it hadn't happened yet.

Lorrie opened her word-processing program and started to write. She'd started this last year, this writing when she felt anxious. Sometimes she used a notebook, though if she was near a computer, she'd work on the keyboard. The teachers called it freewriting, but she didn't know what it was. All she knew was that it made her feel better to rant and rave in this way when she was upset.

It sometimes led to something important, like when she was angry at a teacher once for not giving her the grade she thought she deserved. After the teacher wouldn't change the mark, she complained about it on paper, using all kinds of nasty language to express her sense of injustice. Then she surprised herself by getting some good ideas about her topic that she'd never even thought of for the paper.

And she used to write stupid notes to Barf, notes that she never sent, of course. That would have really been dumb. But she was past that now. Someday she'd read them and laugh.

Tonight she wrote about being here. She wrote about Elaine and her dad and her new short hair. About the pool and Sarah and about meeting Thomas and wishing she were older. And she wrote about meeting Molly and what she hoped to get from working with her. She realized as she typed that she'd been here less than a week and everything about the summer's plans had already changed.

She saved it to a folder named LT, for her initials. Later, after her mom's computer was set up, Lorrie would go back over it and find parts of it to send. She was angry at her mother, but it wouldn't last. It never did.

five

At a quarter to eight on Friday morning, Elaine and Lorrie stood in front of Molly's door. Elaine had already knocked once, and when there had been no response, she lifted her fist and rapped again loudly.

"Aren't we supposed to let ourselves in?" Lorrie said softly, almost whispering. She didn't want to get Molly angry on her first real day on the job.

"I don't have the key yet," Elaine said just as the front door swung open.

"What are you two doing, standing here squawking like jaybirds? Come on in." Molly looked exactly like she had when Lorrie first met her. She wore black slacks and that same green sweater that looked older than Lorrie's dad.

When Molly turned to lead them into the house, Elaine touched Lorrie on the shoulder and playfully mouthed the word "yikes." But Lorrie couldn't manage more than a small smile. She was nervous, and Molly's greeting wasn't helping things.

They'd taken half a dozen very slow steps when Molly

stopped and pulled two keys from her sweater pocket. She handed one to Elaine and thrust the other at Lorrie.

Lorrie stared down at the single key Molly was offering. "I don't need—"

Molly grabbed her hand and deposited the key there. "You're working here now, aren't you? Well, I can't be running to the door every time one of you knocks."

Lorrie couldn't imagine ever coming here alone, but she didn't want to argue with Molly. She jammed the key into the front pocket of her jeans.

Elaine looked around expectantly. "Okay, I'm glad that's settled. Now, where shall we start, Molly?"

"I've made tea," Molly said gruffly.

So they began the morning's work at the kitchen table. Lorrie munched cookies while Molly dawdled over her tea. Lorrie watched her stepmom go through her briefcase of papers and then, finally, give up when Molly wouldn't cooperate. She could see that Molly was just as eager to delay work as Elaine was eager to get started.

Papers aside, Elaine tried a different tactic. "Let's map out a plan for the next few weeks," she said.

Molly sipped her tea and didn't respond.

"We'll start with phase one," Elaine said brightly. "Dealing with the big stuff in each room. The furniture mostly."

Molly didn't answer, so Elaine prompted her. "How does that sound?" To Lorrie, she said, "When Molly moves, her apartment is going to be much smaller than this house, so we need to go through and mark each piece of furniture. Molly can decide what to keep and what needs to go."

Molly set her teacup carefully in its saucer.

Elaine stood up. "I think we can get started now."

Lorrie expected Molly to argue, but she didn't.

In the living room, Elaine handed Lorrie a clipboard. Lorrie's task was to tag each piece of furniture with a number and then record its destination.

"There are probably four choices, don't you think?" Elaine asked Molly, counting off on her fingers as she spoke. "Take it with you, give it away to charity, sell it at auction, or donate it to a museum?"

Molly just grunted in reply. She was gripping the edge of the mantelpiece, and she didn't look happy.

Lorrie put tags on everything in the room and then recorded the numbers on her clipboard, along with a brief description of each piece. The first part of her job done, she waited for Molly to proceed.

It quickly became apparent that this was going to be a long, slow process. Molly had moved away from the mantel and was standing in the middle of the room. She stared at the sofa, and then at the chair, and then at the table by the window. . . . It was as if she were seeing everything in the room for the first time.

Lorrie fought a feeling of impatience. To distract herself, she raised the dusty venetian blind of the living-room window. She climbed onto the wide windowsill and pulled her legs up in front of her.

Outside, a woman from the gas company went from house to house, checking meters. Lorrie watched her until she disappeared up the block. Sighing, Lorrie wondered how on earth she was going to stand a whole summer of this.

Slowly, she became aware of a stillness in the room. The only sound in the house was the ticking of a clock in the upstairs hallway. Her back was to Molly and Elaine, but she could feel them watching her.

Molly was over by the fireplace again, her fingers absently

tracing an obscure design hidden under layers and layers of paint. "Lorrie?"

Startled, Lorrie brought her feet to the ground and held her clipboard out in front of her. This was the first time Molly had addressed her directly.

"I bet you have an opinion about some of these things," the old woman said. "What do you think I should do?"

"Do?"

"Yes. Do. What do you think I should do with that sofa Elaine is sitting on?"

Lorrie looked to Elaine for a rescue, but Elaine, probably exasperated herself, developed a sudden interest in fluffing the pillow beside her.

Molly tried again. "Well, missy, what do you think? Elaine here says I have four choices: take it with me, give it to some stuffy museum, or toss it in the trash. I can't remember the fourth choice."

Lorrie glanced down at her clipboard. "Donate it to charity. And tossing it into the trash isn't one of the choices," she corrected. "Not for the furniture anyway."

"It's not!" Molly exploded. "Then why don't you just tell me what to do with the blooming thing!"

Lorrie was beginning to get annoyed with this whole process. "How should *I* know, Molly? This is *your* stuff."

"I know it's my stuff. I'm asking for your opinion."

"My opinion?"

"My opinion?" Molly parroted.

Lorrie had had enough. She studied the sofa and then shrugged. "In my opinion—" she began, then paused. She started over. "Well, I don't like orange. And when I went to sit on it, it was hard and lumpy, and the fabric is prickly, too." She looked at Molly. "Do you ever sit on it?"

There was a moment of complete silence.

Lorrie held her breath.

All at once, Molly started to chuckle, and then she threw back her head and laughed.

For a moment, Lorrie wasn't sure she was hearing right. It was such a strange sound. She wondered when Molly had last laughed.

Still chuckling, Molly crossed the room and sat down next to Elaine. She ran her hand back and forth across the cushions. "You know, you are absolutely right, my dear," she said. "I've always hated this thing, ever since the day it came in the front door. It belonged to a great-aunt of mine, and I wasn't too fond of her, either. She was a prickly old thing herself." She pointed to the clipboard in Lorrie's hand. "Okay, now, tell me again what my choices are."

Lorrie read from the clipboard.

"Fine. This piece will go to auction. Maybe I'll even make a few dollars off the old thing."

Elaine looked very happy. And a little bit surprised.

"Now let's talk about that footstool over there," Molly said to Lorrie.

Lorrie put down her pen and looked down at it. As far as footstools went, this one was pretty low to the ground. She'd almost tripped over it earlier. "Well," she began, "do you put your feet up on it?"

"Put my feet up on it!" Molly snorted. "It's almost killed me a hundred times."

And so it went. Molly would ask for Lorrie's opinion, and Lorrie would tell her what she thought. Molly didn't always agree, but she didn't seem to be bothered when Lorrie spoke her mind. The pace of the work quickened considerably.

43

Most of the living-room furniture, Molly decided, would be sold at auction. Just a few things—a pair of armchairs and a loveseat and a little wooden table with two chairs off to the side—would stay with Molly. She didn't even discuss these pieces. "Those, I keep," she said without the slightest bit of indecision.

The next room they tackled, the dining room, presented a different problem.

Molly took a seat at the head of the long table. The furniture was dark and heavy. It reminded Lorrie of those *Masterpiece Theatre* dramas on public television.

"My mother gave me this," Molly told Lorrie and Elaine. "It was an anniversary present from Father. That's why I've kept it so long."

Lorrie opened a door of the china cabinet and peeked in. It was packed full with dishes.

"I just don't know," Molly said, sounding pained. "This whole set has been with me my entire adult life."

Elaine, who'd been quiet, spoke up. "It's beautiful, but I'm afraid it's quite large for the apartment you've selected. Look at the height of that cabinet."

All three of them looked up. Elaine was right. The ceilings were high in this house, a couple of feet higher than they'd be in a modern apartment, but even with the added height, the cabinet barely fit the room.

Lorrie opened another cabinet door. "You have a lot of china. Do you like to entertain?"

For the second time this morning, Molly laughed. "Heavens, no! I haven't entertained in years." She fingered the lace tablecloth in her crooked old fingers. "It's been ages since I've had a crowd." Her eyes brightened. "But I did have some fine parties here."

Lorrie picked up a delicate china cup and turned it in her hand. She tried to imagine this dining-room table filled with guests and Molly dressed in something other than that nasty old sweater.

"Molly?" Elaine began. "This is something that a museum would treasure, especially when they learn the family history that comes with it. Let's ask Natalie Dunn for suggestions. The university might have a place for this. I don't know if I told you, Lorrie, there's going to be a room devoted to Molly's work."

Lorrie tried to read the expression on Molly's face as she considered this. Her eyes seemed sad. It had to be hard, Lorrie decided. Giving up your house, your furniture. Even if there was going to be some room somewhere with your name on the door. This work that she and Elaine had come to do must remind Molly that her life was coming to a close, that all these decisions were final ones.

Lorrie thought about all the other stuff in the house. If parting with furniture was so hard, what would it be like when they got to the really personal stuff, like the letters and notebooks and photographs of family and friends? How would that be for Molly? Lorrie herself got sad when she looked at family pictures from ten years ago.

Elaine was starting to say something more when Molly raised a hand. "Lorrie, you can put this down as a possible museum donation. But put a question mark next to it."

Lorrie did as she was told. Day one was over. It hadn't been so bad after all.

· · · · · · · · · · · · · · · · · · · ·

At home, Lorrie found a letter had come from her mom. She took it out to the pool. Just holding the letter in her hand, seeing her mother's loopy, slanting handwriting, made her feel like crying. She brushed the wetness from one eye and tore open the envelope.

"My dear Lorrie," the letter began. "I hope you are all settled in with your dad and Elaine. I think you made a good decision to finish high school there with him (even though I do miss you). But I can't wait for you to visit! This weekend I drove up the coast and saw the seals sitting out on the rocks. The hills are beautiful. I wished you were here to take some pictures for me. You'd love the colors. It's so different from the East Coast. It's hard to explain. And the people are much more laid-back. (Of course, nobody is as intense as the people in Washington.) I am glad I came."

Lorrie smiled. Her mother had hated Bethesda the whole time she was here. This was her dad's town.

The rest of the letter was typical end-of-the-letter stuff, including her mom's address and phone number, which Lorrie already had. "I'll e-mail you when I get set up," she promised. "I miss you and love you," she'd written at the end. "Here's a big hug!"

Lorrie let her eyes go wet without really crying. It was confusing to be angry at her mother but miss her, too. She put the letter aside. She'd write back later. Or maybe send a picture of herself with her new haircut. Her mother would like that. She smiled and began planning in her mind where she'd set up her tripod and timer for the shot.

six

What was I thinking? Lorrie demanded of herself on Sunday morning, realizing now, half an hour before the scheduled lesson with Thomas, that her plan to go all the way over to the stables just to cancel was absurd. At least it was early, and there'd be few other people there. She could talk to Thomas in private, apologize for wasting his time, and be gone.

Sure enough, the stables looked deserted when she pedaled up and locked her bike out front. The parking lot was empty but for two cars.

Even her dislike for horses didn't keep her from enjoying the pretty June morning. Summers in Washington were funny, with some days so hot and humid and the air so polluted that the government declared all buses free so people wouldn't drive their cars, and others as beautiful and clear as an early-spring day. Today was one of those beautiful cool days.

Her lesson wasn't for another couple of minutes. Lorrie was in no hurry to enter the barn. She leaned against the railing of the back pen and rested her chin in her hands.

Two horses stood together, their noses almost touching. Their honey-colored coats shone in the still, sunny air.

"Hello there."

Lorrie jumped at the sound of Thomas's voice. Her smile felt too wide. She was nervous, and his sudden appearance made it worse. He was even better-looking than she remembered, especially this morning, when his jeans and gray T-shirt seemed so fresh and clean. He was taller than she recalled, too.

He was waiting for her to speak. She said the first thing she could think of. "It's a beautiful day, isn't it?" And then she wanted to kick herself for talking about something as dumb as the weather.

But Thomas lifted his face into the sunshine and then looked back at her, smiling easily. "It's funny how much the horses are affected by the weather. Look how calm they are today. When it's humid, they're all out of sorts, just like the rest of us." He gestured toward the open stable door. "The horse I have for you isn't nearly as pretty as these two, or as fast, but I think you'll like her."

"Thomas—" Lorrie stopped. She wondered if that was what she was supposed to call him. She didn't call teachers by their first names, but this had to be different. "I should have contacted you earlier. You see, I can't—"

"Can't pay? I told Sarah there was no charge. Sometimes I give lessons for free, especially when the rider is really fearful. I like doing that," he explained with a smile.

"No, no, it's not the money. It's just that—"

"Did you know that Sarah feels responsible for your fall?" he interrupted. "I told her, of course, that she was being ridiculous, but she feels tremendously guilty."

"She had nothing to do with it," Lorrie protested. But even as she said this, she remembered Sarah's part in the day. The horse had been skittish, and Lorrie hadn't wanted to ride, but Sarah had insisted, and so she had climbed up on him anyway. She had never held anything against Sarah—it certainly wasn't her friend's fault that when the horse reared she had lost control.

"At least come in and meet Niki," Thomas was saying. "She's been looking forward to meeting you all morning."

"Niki?"

"Your horse. I've told her all about you."

It was so silly, pretending that the horse was waiting for her, that Lorrie followed him into the darkened doorway of the barn.

"Over here," Thomas called.

Lorrie's eyes adjusted to the light, and she started laughing. The small white horse beside Thomas was the most decrepit-looking thing she'd ever seen. "*That's* my horse?"

Thomas put a finger to his lips and shot her a mock frown. "She's younger than she looks," he whispered.

"She is not!" The little horse was ancient.

"Okay, she's not," Thomas said, smiling. "But she's wonderful with beginners. Now, come on. You've ridiculed her long enough."

Lorrie did feel a little unkind, particularly when Niki's big brown eyes looked into hers.

Thomas handed her a brush. "I always include grooming as part of the lesson. It lets you get used to each other."

Lorrie took a tentative step forward.

"I've got to go over something with Shane in the office. Go ahead and get started," he said. And then he was gone.

Lorrie looked at the brush and then at Niki. She didn't know if a horse could really look inquisitive, but if one could, this one sure did. "All right, all right, I'm getting to it." She stepped over and put the brush lightly on the horse's curved back. Niki shifted about, startling Lorrie. She was almost back out the barn door when she realized how silly she was being. She tiptoed up to the horse again. "Niki," she said, softly, "what's an old horse like you doing in a place like this?" She was anxious, but maybe if she kept talking it would be all right.

She rested the brush on Niki's back and slowly moved it downward. Niki turned her head, and Lorrie froze. A moment passed, and then another. Again, Lorrie felt as though this horse were questioning her with those big brown eyes of hers, but when she didn't do anything more than stare—when she didn't rear up on her hind legs or do any other crazy thing that Lorrie could easily imagine—Lorrie started to relax. She continued brushing. This time, Niki stood still, and Lorrie slowly got into a rhythm. When Thomas returned, she told him, "I think she likes this."

"Of course she likes it. And I think she likes you, too."

"You didn't tell me you were the manager here."

"You didn't ask."

"I thought you were an instructor, like Sarah."

"I am. They just have me doing the paperwork, too."

"And in the fall, when you go to college?"

"I've got my classes scheduled for mornings, and I'll be here in the afternoons." He shrugged. "I'm going to have to see how it goes."

Lorrie brushed some tangles out of Niki's white mane.

"Ready for the fun part?" Thomas grabbed a blanket and saddle. "Lend me a hand," he said, not waiting for an answer.

The last time Lorrie had saddled a horse was the day she was thrown. Thomas handed her the reins, and she stared down at them, running the rough leather through her fingers and remembering.

"Take her into the ring while *I* saddle up," he said.

"Umm. I don't think Niki feels like riding today," she began.

"Niki always feels like riding. She's the Energizer Bunny."

Lorrie looked at the little horse with her swayed back. Her days as an Energizer anything were long gone.

Thomas nudged Niki toward the empty ring, and it was easier for Lorrie to follow the horse than to stop her.

The sawdust on the floor here was a foot deep. That reassured Lorrie but scared her, too. People must be falling on it all the time, she decided as Niki led her to the center of the ring.

Thomas's black horse was huge. "What do you say we just lead our horses around a little bit and you tell me what you remember about riding?" he asked her.

Walking their horses was actually kind of fun. There didn't seem to be much threat of danger after Niki fell into step beside the black horse, leaving Lorrie and Thomas to walk ahead of them, side by side. Just when Lorrie was hoping that they could do this for the remainder of the lesson time, Thomas pulled his horse to a stop.

"Okay. Time to ride," he said. "We'll ride at this same pace. Need a boost up?"

Niki was small, but not so small that Lorrie could just hop right on her without the danger of going up and over the other side.

Thomas sensed her hesitation. "I'll steady her," he said, dropping his own reins and coming over.

Up in the saddle, Lorrie looked down to the ground.

Niki wasn't big by anybody's standards, but it would still be a long way to fall.

"You're doing great," Thomas called from his horse. Now, *he* was high up. "Just follow my lead."

That wasn't hard to do. The old horse fell into step behind Thomas's horse and just stayed there. Lorrie sat in her saddle and tried to remember everything she'd ever learned about riding. Every so often, Thomas would look back to see how she was doing.

She was just beginning to relax when Thomas stopped his horse and grabbed Niki's bridle. "Listen, Lorrie. Normally, I'd quit here for the day and have you brush down Niki in her stall, but I was wondering if you'd like to go and check the trails with me. Sometimes branches fall across the paths, and it's my job to go out and make sure everything is clear before we get our Sunday riding groups out there. Will you come along?" He grinned and added, "It's one of Niki's favorite things to do."

Lorrie smiled down at her horse. "It's nice of you to ask, but I don't think so. I think I've done enough for the day."

"Please come," he said simply.

Lorrie lifted the stiff white hair of Niki's mane and let it run through her fingers.

"It's solid ground the whole way."

Lorrie considered it. When she'd fallen, it had been off the trail and deep in the woods. She petted the warm neck of her gentle old horse. So far, this hadn't been bad.

"Follow me," Thomas said, taking her silence as a yes.

Niki didn't share Lorrie's indecision. Eagerly, she followed the other horse from the barn.

After five minutes out on the trail, Lorrie could see there was nothing to worry about. Thomas had set a slow, easy pace, and the path beneath them was solid dirt, with no holes or rough spots that a horse could trip on. It was nothing like the woodsy trail where she had fallen.

She was glad she'd come. She had developed a quick affection for Niki, and Thomas's horse, though big, seemed harmless enough. "Is that your own horse?" she asked Thomas when he pulled back to ride beside her.

"Who, Bullet here?"

"Bullet? His name is Bullet?"

"I didn't name him. My grandpa bought him off an owner who had raced him."

"*Raced him?*" Now that she was taking a second look, Lorrie could see that he wasn't your ordinary stable horse. "Then he's fast."

"Oh, yeah. He's fast all right." Thomas patted Bullet on the neck. "Aren't you, boy?" He turned in his saddle and grinned at Lorrie. "Want a demonstration?"

Lorrie's fingers tightened around the reins, and her legs squeezed Niki's sides. "No, I do not think so," she said, emphasizing each word.

Thomas laughed, then looked at her sober expression and laughed all over again. But he kept his horse at a walk.

seven

By the end of the second day at Molly's, Lorrie felt more comfortable with Molly's gruff style and her excruciatingly slow way of doing things. When the old photographer shuffled through the rooms ever so slowly, or took a long moment or two before speaking, Lorrie found herself able to wait quietly without wanting to rush her. It was a little bit like being in school, sitting through the frequent moments of inactivity in the classroom, those times when the teacher got the holes punched in papers or recorded grades in the gradebook.

But Molly's was much better than school. It felt at times like Lorrie was working in an art gallery, with all those pictures on the walls. Whenever things slowed down and she knew she'd have to wait, Lorrie studied the framed photos that were everywhere. Many of the shots had writing on them, notes Molly had written or autographs of the person in the picture. There was one of President Jimmy Carter with this inscription: "Molly, you've been wonderful to work with. Thank you for your professionalism and your spirit!"

Spirit? Lorrie looked over at Molly, who stood next to a tall dresser in a small study off the kitchen where she napped sometimes on a daybed. Lorrie tried to imagine her as she might have been years ago, back in the 1970s, when Carter was president. Molly with dark brown hair and legs that were quick and strong. It was hard to picture. This Molly, in her green sweater despite the summer heat, had been standing in front of that dresser for the last five minutes, yanking open drawers and lifting the drawer pulls up and dropping them while she considered where this piece of furniture might go.

························

By midweek, the three of them had finished downstairs. They climbed up the turning staircase and entered what Molly referred to as her office.

Lorrie fell in love with it as soon as she stepped inside. Unlike the dreary rooms on the first floor, dark and over-crowded with furniture no one ever used, this sunny place looked lived-in and alive. The pale yellow walls made the room feel warm, and the blues and reds of the braided rug brought color into the space. The windows faced the back of the house, and one of them had a deep window seat filled with thick, soft cushions. Here, unlike anywhere else in the house, hung pots of vibrant green plants.

Elsewhere, downstairs at least, the surfaces of furniture were covered with dingy old doilies, but here Molly's desk was cluttered with the papers and trinkets of a traveler. A snow dome of the Eiffel Tower, a moose coffee cup from Canada, a small gargoyle from some ancient rooftop.

But the best part of the room was the pictures. Molly's photographs covered every inch of the walls and were propped up against books on the shelves.

Most everything here would stay with her, Molly quickly decided. But because the room was so sunny and comfortable, it became the place the three of them took their breaks. Lorrie would climb into the window seat, Elaine would fold up in the chintz-covered chair, and Molly would sit in the big swivel chair behind the desk.

They worked well together, Lorrie decided. She and Elaine paced themselves to Molly's speed and crankiness. Lorrie was even starting to tease her a little bit, making small jokes that Molly and Elaine smiled at.

....

Toward the end of that first week, Lorrie found herself alone with Molly for the first time. Their routine was to break for tea at ten, which Lorrie usually made, but this time it was Elaine who went to the kitchen. A case at work hadn't been going well, and she had been paged twice this morning already. Through the open doorway of Molly's office, Lorrie could hear Elaine on the kitchen phone.

Without Elaine in the room, Lorrie, snuggled up against the cool glass of the window, suddenly felt awkward with Molly. One of those uncomfortable silences had fallen, and Lorrie could think of nothing to say. She wasn't like Sarah, who was never at a loss for words.

Lorrie thought of asking Molly about one of the photos, but Molly had been grouchy all morning and had even snapped at Elaine earlier, when her pager went off for the second time. "Which job are you working?" she had demanded—rudely, Lorrie thought. Elaine had apologized, but then left the room to make tea and call the office.

Finally, unable to stand the silence any longer, Lorrie stood up and stretched her arms above her head to get the stiffness of the early morning out of her body. Pretending to take a sudden interest in a certain photograph, she stepped over to examine it. Quickly, as always, her interest became genuine. She forgot all about Molly and making conversation.

Molly's voice startled her. "You spend a lot of time staring at my pictures," she barked. "What do you think of them?"

"Think of them?" Lorrie repeated dumbly.

"Good Lord, missy. You got a hearing problem? Just answer the question."

Lorrie was flustered. She couldn't just answer the question. "Uh, well," she began to mumble, "I think they're great. I think your pictures are wonderful."

Molly scrunched up her face in disgust. "What is that? You've been examining them for the past ten minutes," she said, sounding like a teacher drilling a cocky student, "so surely you have an opinion. I'm curious. What do you think? And say something, not just that they are great." She made "great" sound like a bad word.

Lorrie wished Elaine would walk in now with the tea, but Lorrie could hear her downstairs on the phone, arguing with someone. Everyone was cranky today.

She walked over to the wall nearest her, looking at one picture and then another, searching for the right words to say. Molly leaned back in her chair and waited.

Lorrie pushed what was left of her hair up off her forehead. It was an old habit, but she was nervous. Why on earth would Molly Price, a photographer whose pictures were famous all over the world, care what some kid thought of her work?

The grandfather clock outside the door ticked aloud the minutes. Molly's blue eyes were on her. Lorrie started to feel annoyed. *Okay,* she thought, *I'll just tell her what I think. If I say something stupid, who cares? Maybe she'll learn not to ask.*

She went to one of her favorites. It was a picture of the same guy she'd seen in the photo downstairs by the back door, the man holding the gardening hat.

This time, the man, dressed up in a suit like men wore in the 1940s, was stretched out on a lumpy blanket with the high grass of a field behind him. Beside him were an open picnic basket, plates and silverware, and the remains of a lunch. He was leaning back on his elbows, his long legs in their baggy dress slacks extended out in front of him. One of his feet was resting in a plate of ham.

Lorrie chuckled.

"What's so funny?" Molly demanded.

Lorrie had, for a second, forgotten about her. "It's the ham," she said, smiling. "The way his foot is in it and he doesn't even know. He looks so oblivious. He has a look on his face of complete contentment. You know?"

Molly leaned forward, focusing her old, watery eyes on the shot. Her face broke into a smile as she said, "Yes, that's right. I'd forgotten that."

Lorrie pointed to another photo, a smaller one that Molly would have a hard time seeing from where she sat. "And this one, too," she said, speaking over her shoulder to Molly. "The one of the girls on the beach, building the sand castle." The castle was high and sloppily built. A young girl of about five held a shovel full of sand above it. She looked delighted with what she was about to do.

"When you look at the shot," continued Lorrie, "you just know what's going to happen next."

"Yes, I do," admitted Molly. "I remember it well." Her

glance moved from that shot to another, and another. "I remember them all. Everything."

Lorrie thought about this and realized it was true for her, too. When she took pictures of her family, not good pictures like Molly's but pictures the family treasured, she remembered everything about the moment for years afterward.

Molly leaned forward on the desk, her gaze fixed on Lorrie. "I'm not sure you answered me. What is it about these pictures that you like?"

"What I *like*," said Lorrie, looking back at Molly, "is that, when you look at the picture, you see what's there, of course, but then, in your mind, you get to see *another* shot." She pointed to the picnic photo. "You just know that this guy is going to suddenly discover his foot is in the ham and he will hop up and apologize and maybe"—she said, turning to study his handsome face—"maybe he will get all flustered and embarrassed for being so clumsy. And the girls. Well, you know that this shovel of sand is going to collapse the castle that they are both so happy with. And you can see, in your mind, the picture of them looking all shocked and disappointed."

She studied the photos a little longer before turning around. "It's like you've given us two pictures at once. The one that's here and the one that automatically appears in our minds. That's what I like," she concluded. "The shot engages."

Molly was quiet. Lorrie kept talking. "I never thought to do this. When I take a picture, I—"

"You? You take pictures?"

Quickly, Lorrie shook her head. "Oh, no. Not like that," she protested. "Not like you do. You know how in every family there's one person who takes the pictures? I'm that person. But my pictures, well, mine are all posed. Everyone just says 'cheese,' and I snap the shot."

Molly had an odd look on her face. "Do you develop your own film?" she asked.

"Not the color shots. But at my old school—I did take some pictures there for the school paper." She hesitated while she considered telling Molly about the shot that made it into the *Clearfield News*. She was thinking about it, about what Molly would think of this achievement, when Molly's next words caught her completely off guard.

"I have a darkroom here that you're welcome to use, if you'd like."

Lorrie's mouth slowly dropped open. Had she heard right?

"A darkroom," Molly repeated. "There's a darkroom down in the basement. It belonged to the man in the picnic shot, Albert Blake. I haven't used it in years, but, if you want to get in there and clean it up, go right ahead."

Lorrie was stunned. "Really? You mean it?"

"I just said so, didn't I?"

At that moment, Elaine walked in, holding the tea tray out in front of her. "I'm sorry I took so long." She was frowning, still upset about the argument she'd just had.

Lorrie and Molly's conversation came to an abrupt end.

Lorrie heard nothing from that point on, as Elaine and Molly talked over plans for the rest of the morning. All she could think of was the darkroom. Molly Price's darkroom!

She was jolted out of this reverie by the sharp tone that had come into Elaine's voice. "I know you don't want to do it *now*, Molly, but how about giving me some indication of *when*?" She sounded totally frustrated. "Just give me a date

I can work with. This process involves a lot of paperwork. Much more than you seem to think. I can't just call Natalie Dunn one day and say, Okay, we're ready now. Come on over." Elaine folded her arms across her chest. "It doesn't work like that. For one thing, it's rude."

Lorrie picked up the snow dome and turned it over. She'd never heard Elaine angry. The snowflakes fell down over the tower and landed softly on the ground. She turned it over again.

Molly stood up and leaned over the desk toward Elaine. "I don't care if it's rude," she spat. "I don't care one bit. Now, if you will excuse me, I've had enough for the day. I'm feeling tired." She slowly made her way to the door, her head held high, looking intimidating in a little-old-lady sort of way. Like if she had an umbrella she'd swat you with it. "And shut that door behind you," she barked as she left the room. "I'm spending a fortune on this blooming air-conditioning."

Lorrie expected Elaine to say something, to try to make peace, but Elaine only said, "We'll see you tomorrow."

When the door to Molly's bedroom was shut behind her, Elaine spoke in a low voice. "Don't let what just happened bother you, Lorrie. Molly's a mature, responsible woman, and I'm not doing her any favors if I baby her. She's got decisions that need to be made. There's no way around it."

Lorrie knew that Elaine was right, but she just wished she hadn't chosen today to argue. Lorrie hadn't finished talking to Molly about the darkroom, and now, with everything left unsettled, she wasn't even sure that Molly had been serious.

eight

But later that day, when she had thought some more about it, Lorrie realized that the idea of the darkroom could work with or without Molly. Here, at her dad and Elaine's, there was a basement bathroom that hardly got used. It would be easy to cover up the window and work in there. It was small, but it had the essentials: darkness and water.

She stood in the dusty little room and tried to remember what else went into a darkroom. The one at school had been set up and ready to go. Surely there were books on this in the Bethesda library.

....

She was right. When she got there, she discovered a whole shelf on photography. Lorrie grabbed everything that had "darkroom" in the title and spread her stuff out on one of the wide tables. She looked around the place while she got herself settled. It hadn't changed much in all the years she'd been coming here, starting with those story hours her mom had brought Sarah and her to.

She wasn't far into the first book when she knew she'd

be able to do it. Setting up a darkroom wasn't that complicated. She flipped through the books, choosing the ones with the clearest directions and photos to illustrate.

It was cool in the library, and Lorrie wasn't eager to go back outside. The air was much stickier and dirtier here than it'd been in Clearfield, and she was glad there was a pool to throw herself into later. Returning to the photography section, she pulled out a few books and plopped down on the floor with them. Ansel Adams. Mathew Brady. So many good American photographers to study.

That's when she saw it, down near the bottom of the shelf. *The Photography of Molly Price.*

"Oh, wow!" she cried. An entire book, and a big one, too, all about Molly!

Her heart pounding, she took it from the shelf and opened it. It was one of those oversized books with shiny pages. Lots of shiny pages, all of them filled with Molly's work.

She flipped through slowly, seeing here, there, everywhere, the shots she'd been looking at on Molly's walls.

"Gosh," she whispered to herself. There were the girls building the sand castle! And there were the shots of the soldier who died in Vietnam!

Lorrie held the book against her chest and turned back to the shelf. There were other books about Molly, a whole bunch of them. She stacked them up and carried them back over to the table.

Opening book after book, Lorrie saw hundreds of photos that Molly had taken over her long career, which had ended, as far as Lorrie could tell, about ten or fifteen years ago. As Lorrie had guessed from Molly's house, Molly mostly liked to take pictures of people, people engaged in doing something.

Lorrie thought about what wasn't in these books. She

didn't see many nature shots. No flowers or landscapes, like some of the other notable photographers she knew. Molly didn't have many war pictures. Only a bunch from Vietnam, but nothing from any later conflicts.

There was one picture Lorrie returned to again and again. It was a shot of Molly, taken when she was young. She stood tall and thin, and her hair was wavy and parted on the side, forties-style. Only her face, with its angular nose and don't-give-me-any-nonsense eyes, looked like Molly. This woman was strong and agile, standing on the peak of a gravelly mountaintop, her tripod set up beside her, a camera around her neck.

Lorrie thought of the Molly who wore Keds that slipped on like loafers and an old green sweater with the middle button missing. It was no fair, this getting old.

....

Late that night, long after the house was quiet, Lorrie sat cross-legged on her bed with Molly's work all about her in books she'd brought home to show her father and Elaine. She would never look at Molly the same way again.

Molly had spent weeks in the dusty fields of Oklahoma shooting pictures of migrant families, she'd lived in Harlem during the civil-rights era, and she'd been to Vietnam. She'd taken pictures of every president since she was twenty— and that covered quite a few. She'd shot in every major city in the country, and had been to Paris, to Prague, and to Rome, where she had photographed the Pope. She'd gone to Africa, to the Arctic, to the jungles of South America.

Lorrie lay back on her pillow. What an exciting life!

She was thinking about all this when her gaze fell on one of the open books at her side. There was the same guy whose foot was in the ham! He wasn't in the garden or out on the blanket having a picnic. He was in a restaurant with a woman, not Molly, at his side.

Lorrie sat up. She was suddenly extremely curious.

Information was surprisingly sketchy, just his name, Albert Blake, and not much more. How strange. Why had he been in Molly's backyard, and why did he have a dark-room in her basement?

At last Lorrie found a tiny bit of information in an end-note in one of the books. Albert Blake was married to a woman from one of New York's richest families. He and his wife were both friends with Molly, but a rumor persisted that there was something more between Albert Blake and Molly Price. That's all the brief endnote said.

Elaine had been right. Though Molly's pictures were on display for all the world to see, her personal life was another matter entirely.

Lorrie gathered up the books and deposited them on her desk. They had thoroughly covered Molly's career. Her published pictures for news agencies all around the country made tracking her professional life very easy to do. But where was Molly's story?

If there was little in these books about Albert Blake, there was even *less* about Molly's childhood. Lorrie couldn't remember reading much at all about Molly's parents or her sister who'd died when Molly was five. Nor had the books contained any mention of Molly's childhood dog, Sweater, or of the time Molly pulled over the pot of hot creamed-potato soup and badly burned her mother's leg.

And where was the story of Molly's aunt who was put in a sanitarium, or the story of Hope, Molly's first business partner and favorite cousin? Molly had actually cried when she'd talked about this woman, who'd died five years ago, and whose funeral Molly still regretted missing.

Lorrie could see why Elaine was so frustrated with Molly's reluctance to talk to someone like that university professor. These stories, which Molly was telling freely to Lorrie and Elaine each day, were wonderful. Lorrie wished that others could hear them, too. She decided to try to write them down. Maybe she could share them with Sarah sometime later.

Lorrie booted up her computer and opened her free-writing file. Writing was easy for her, especially this kind of writing, where no teacher would be coming behind to put on a grade. She wrote page after page, not worrying about the grammar or the paragraphs until she was done.

When she couldn't write any more, she saved the file with the title "The Stories of Molly Price." And then she went back and read over the whole thing, adding details and, where she could recall Molly's words, exact quotes. This was fun, and very different from anything Lorrie had ever done.

Of course, nothing she'd written sounded as scholarly as what she'd read in the books from the library, but the stories were good. And, more important, nobody had ever heard them before.

She wondered if this was how her dad felt when he oversaw the production of an exhibit down at the Smithsonian. Documenting the life of someone important so that the details of that life wouldn't be lost. When the summer was over, maybe she'd clean up the entire document, put it into chapters or something, and give a copy to the reclusive photographer.

The next morning, work at Molly's house got a lot harder. The decisions about furniture were done, and it was time for Molly to figure out what to do with all the rest of her belongings.

It wasn't going to be easy, Lorrie quickly realized. Fifty years' worth of books, clothes, papers, and photographs—this was worse than cleaning your closet a hundred times over, she decided.

Molly agonized over every item, turning it over and over in her hands. Lorrie couldn't help her with this part. Every decision felt momentous, and Molly was easily exhausted.

After reading those library books yesterday, Lorrie was more curious than ever about her. She knew that when Molly held a childhood picture book or an old postcard in her hand she was remembering things, things Lorrie wanted to hear. It didn't take too much prodding to get Molly to talk, and as Lorrie expected, this old woman who'd traveled all over the world had a tale to go with everything. Ignoring Elaine's puzzled looks, Lorrie asked questions—and memorized names and details and dates so that she could go home and write them all down.

Late Friday morning, after several slow hours of this tedious work, Elaine's office beeped her with an urgent request that she come in to work. Lorrie could see the obvious relief on Molly's face when Elaine apologized profusely for having to quit early that day.

Lorrie was preparing to leave with her when Molly stopped her. "Lorrie, you never gave me an answer on that darkroom."

"An answer?"

"Yes, are you interested?"

Lorrie was more than interested! "Yes," she said, waving good-bye to Elaine, who was hurrying out the door, her cell phone at her ear.

Lorrie held the old woman's arm as they descended the

wooden staircase into the unfinished basement. Did Molly ever come down here anymore?

If she did, she certainly didn't go into the darkroom. Lorrie had to move boxes stacked in front of the door and push through cobwebs to get in. She flipped on the light. The room obviously hadn't been touched in years. It was dirty and dusty and dark. The small sink was full of dead bugs, and the countertops and cabinet fronts were stained and streaked with old chemicals and dirt. The old black dial phone on the wall was white with dust.

Lorrie didn't care. Brushing off the dust, she pulled a work stool into the center of the room for Molly. "Here. Sit down and tell me about this," she said, reaching for Molly's arm to stabilize her.

From her perch, Molly looked all about her. "I never much cared for this part," she sniffed.

Lorrie thought that all photographers liked darkroom work, but when she said as much, Molly laughed. "No, this was Albert's room."

Lorrie wanted to know more. "Albert?" She tried to make her voice sound casual, like she wasn't really interested at all.

Molly wasn't easily fooled. "Albert Blake," she said crossly. "I already told you his name. He was a friend of mine. I did have friends, missy. You think you know a lot about me, you and Elaine, but you don't."

Lorrie didn't protest or react to the cross tone. She was getting used to Molly's manner and knew when to let things pass.

Molly pointed to a drawer. "He might have left some of his work here," she said. "He was always taking pictures of flowers. So many pictures of flowers. Lord, you'd think he'd tire of it, but he never did."

Lorrie looked at Molly in surprise. Albert Blake—the mystery man, as she was starting to think of him—had left his work right here in this darkroom! Excitedly she began pulling out drawers and opening cabinets, but all she found were old jars of chemicals and more dead bugs.

Lorrie decided to tell Molly what little she did know about the mystery man. "I read about Albert Blake in a book. I saw a picture of him, in fact."

Molly snorted. "What book?"

Lorrie turned to face her. Molly didn't intimidate her anymore. "Something I found at the library. I read that you were friends, but I didn't read anything about him having a darkroom here."

Molly got that mean look she wore when she was disgusted. "The people who wrote those books knew nothing," she declared, standing up. "Here you are. I've shown you the place. You'll have to make do if you like it. I'm going upstairs to take a nap," she said, moving slowly toward the open door.

At the bottom of the staircase, Lorrie took her arm and helped her up the steps. "Molly," she said, "you mean I can fix it up and use it?"

"Suit yourself. It's filthy."

"I know. But I can clean it."

They were almost at the top. Molly paused to rest.

"Can I start now?"

Molly chuckled. "Yes, dear, you can start now. There's cleaning supplies under that kitchen sink. The mop is in the broom closet."

"Thank you so much." Impulsively, Lorrie reached over and kissed her on the cheek. "You are so sweet."

"Oh, pooh," Molly protested, but her eyes were soft when she said it. She pulled out of Lorrie's grasp and shuffled toward the small study where she napped during the day.

....

Lorrie had never attempted to clean a room that was quite this dirty. The soapy water in the bucket had to be changed repeatedly until she had gone over every part of the room twice.

Her father was the one who had taught her how to clean. Remembering his instructions, she started with the ceiling and worked her way down. She worked slowly, spending hours washing out the trays and the measuring bottles and thoroughly wiping down the machines. Finally, all that was left was one last mopping of the floor.

Lorrie stood in the doorway, admiring her work. The walls and cabinets really could have used some fresh paint, but she was only a guest here. Besides, the lights would be out. It was, after all, a darkroom.

She couldn't wait to buy her supplies. She wished she could already drive . . . but she was getting ahead of herself. She didn't even know what she needed.

Lorrie found Molly up on the second floor, in her office, sitting at her desk, sorting through an old box of photos. She handed one to Lorrie. "My mother," she said.

The woman looked a little bit like Molly around the eyes, but she could have been anybody's mother from the turn of the century. This stern-looking lady wore what was probably her nicest dress. Her hair was back in a bun, and a string of pearls circled her neck. But the hoe leaning up against the old fence gave her away. She was a working woman who dressed this way for church and funerals—and visiting photographers. Lorrie studied the picture before handing it back, memorizing details to add to her story file at home.

The next thing Molly put in Lorrie's hands was a list of darkroom supplies. The old-fashioned handwriting reminded her of her grandmother's spidery script. "This will get you started," Molly said, thrusting an envelope at her. Lorrie knew instantly it was money. She could feel the wad of it, folded in half and secured with a rubber band.

Molly wasn't the only one who could be stubborn. Lorrie shoved the envelope back into the old photographer's hands and, when that failed, dropped it into the pocket of her green sweater. "No way, Molly. Not a chance."

"You don't know how costly this business of a darkroom can be," Molly protested.

"I don't care. I am *not* taking money from you." Lorrie crossed her arms against her chest. "Ain't no way."

"Ain't no way," Molly mimicked. And then, softening her voice just a little, she said, "You must know that Elaine is setting up scholarships for me with the money I have in my estate. I am very comfortable financially. I would like to think of this as a scholarship."

"This *isn't* a scholarship. If that was your intent, you should have said so right from the beginning, before I got started. I am not going to take your money."

Molly eyed her for several long moments. "You are a stubborn one."

"Same goes for you," Lorrie said, lifting her chin but not breaking their gaze.

And then they both laughed. Molly put the envelope into the top drawer of her desk. "Hand me back that list. There's something I forgot. You'll need a big sheet of paper. What's that paper called that children use for school projects?"

"Posterboard?"

"Yes, although any big sheet will do. Now sit down for a

minute. I want to tell you a few things so you don't go into the shop this weekend a total beginner."

"I *am* a beginner," said Lorrie, taking a seat in the chintz-covered chair. "But give me a couple weeks."

"You sound pretty sure of yourself."

Lorrie shrugged. She could be a quick study if she liked something.

"Okay, now, let's see how well you listen. I'm going to tell you what *not* to buy."

Lorrie grabbed a pen and pad off the desk. "Shoot," she said.

Molly chuckled, and Lorrie smiled back. Molly was enjoying this as much as she was.

nine

Lorrie's second fight about money was with her dad. This one was harder to win.

"It'll be such a wonderful opportunity," he said late Friday afternoon, as they pulled into the parking lot of Penn Camera. "I really never imagined when you took this job that you'd be learning photography from Molly Price."

"I'm not, Dad," Lorrie insisted. She hated the way everything was an opportunity. Why couldn't anything just be for fun?

Then he was talking about school again. "This could dovetail nicely with your history curriculum," he said.

Dovetail with her curriculum? She couldn't believe he'd just said that. They were standing on the sidewalk in front of the store. She turned to him and grabbed his arm before he opened the door. "You know, Dad, if you're going to make such a big deal out of it, I'm not going to do it."

"A big deal out of it? What are you talking about?" He really didn't know.

"Look, this is just something I want to do for me. That's why I want to pay for it. It's not for school. It's not a wonderful opportunity. It's just something that I think I might enjoy."

"Okay," he said slowly.

"When we get in here, please let me handle it. Molly told me exactly what I need, and I have it all written down. Please, Dad. I'll let you know if you can help."

A moment passed while he considered her words. "Okay," he said again, sounding slightly baffled. "I don't know what this is about, but you're on your own."

True to his word, he stayed out of the way. As soon as they got into the store, he went over to the photocopier machine and pulled a small picture of Lorrie out of his wallet. While she talked to the sales guy, her dad played with the machine, enlarging and cropping the snapshot until he had a print he was pleased with.

Nobody even realized they were together until it was time to pay.

"Molly was right. It's expensive," Lorrie admitted when the total came to more than two hundred dollars. She pulled out her wallet. "I'm working now," she said, giving her father a look that said, *Don't argue with me.* She knew her father would do something crazy like put an equal amount in her college fund or something, but for now she had won.

He was quiet as they loaded the bags into the back seat. She thought perhaps she had made him angry or hurt his feelings somehow, but if she had, he didn't show it. Instead, he began, as he drove, to talk to her about work. He was setting up a new exhibit at the museum and was considering an interactive display. "It's one of those computerized things. The display is just about complete, but there are parts to it that just don't work the way I'd like them to. I was hoping that you could come down one afternoon next week and take a look. I'd be interested in hearing what you think. Maybe bring Sarah along."

"Sure, Dad." Lorrie liked this sort of thing. Ever since she was little, her dad had included her in his work. She'd grown up behind the scenes, meeting historians, watching how his staff labored over every exhibit. She and Sarah loved exploring the back rooms of the Smithsonian.

"Come down late on Wednesday, and then we'll take the subway home together."

"Sounds great," she said. "I'll talk to Sarah tonight."

· · · · · · · · · · · · · · · · · · ·

Lorrie spread her darkroom supplies out in front of her on her bedroom floor and, with the help of one of the books, ran through in her mind the whole process of developing and printing. She read the box that the black-and-white film came in. She couldn't wait to take her first pictures.

But when she got up the next morning, it was pouring rain. Instead of going out with her camera, Lorrie spent all of Saturday afternoon hanging around at Sarah's house, because Sarah had to baby-sit her little sister. Their parents had a wedding to go to.

Deciding not to waste a day, Lorrie brought along her camera and set up a "studio" in the O'Connells' bathroom. She hung a white sheet over the shower curtain and brought two stools in from the kitchen. Against this background, she took pictures of Sarah and Amy and their funny-looking dog, Einstein.

The three of them started off serious, but after a while they got silly. Sarah and Amy put on their dad's suits and their mother's evening gowns and dressed up the dog, too.

Then they decided to keep the whole thing a secret so they could surprise Sarah's parents with the developed pictures. Their twentieth wedding anniversary was in late July, and Lorrie was sure that by then she'd know everything there was to know about making prints.

Later that evening, after her parents had returned, Sarah talked Lorrie into going out with some of her friends to a new coffeehouse down in Georgetown. "You have to meet Joel," Sarah insisted.

Joel wasn't anything like the other guys Sarah had dated. For one thing, he smoked. For another, he wore leather pants. Lorrie didn't know anyone in Clearfield who wore leather pants. But he was friendly and easy to talk to. It was clear that Sarah adored him. Lorrie had never seen her so quiet around a boyfriend. And so physical. All night, she'd kept her hand in his, and she must have leaned over and kissed him a couple of dozen times.

The rest of the group was more typical of the friends Sarah had always had, and Lorrie knew some of them already. They were the kids from the honors classes—smart, but not the top students in school. Most of the girls were on the field-hockey team, and the boys played soccer. A lot played lacrosse in the spring. Some, like Sarah, took band or were in school plays. It was a fun, busy crowd, not that different from Lorrie's friends in Clearfield, though no one in this bunch was on the school paper.

Sarah and her friends tried to include Lorrie in the conversation, but they'd all just done the school year together, and it was hard to feel a part of things when everything they talked about had happened at Whitman last year.

Lorrie hadn't been to the spring dance or taken any of the final exams. She hadn't gone to the basketball game where the riot almost broke out, and she hadn't had the chemistry teacher who'd been arrested for driving the getaway car for a holdup at a 7-Eleven. Sarah had told her about all these things, but that wasn't the same.

At eleven, when the group decided to leave the coffeehouse and go to someone's house to listen to music and shoot pool, Lorrie asked Joel to drop her at home. She had an early riding lesson, she explained. She ignored Sarah's teasing questions about Thomas.

•••••••••••••••••••••

Sunday was a perfect day for shooting. The rain had left the air clear and clean, and the famous Washington humidity that left the horizon smudged and blurry was gone today. Lorrie decided to take her camera along to her lesson.

Early again, she came upon Thomas in the back pen with the horses. He was examining the hoof of a chocolate-brown horse named Kiss.

Lorrie lifted her camera to her eye, playing with the zoom lens, bringing Thomas in to fill the frame. She didn't like to take pictures of people secretly, so she waited until Thomas saw her and waved. Most people would have reacted to the camera, but it didn't seem to bother him. She gestured at it, silently asking him with a tilt of her head whether it was okay.

Then she got serious. She snapped frame after frame, changing the settings both to under- and to overexpose, so that she'd be sure to get a good shot. The teacher in charge of the paper last year had taught her to do this. "It's called bracketing," he'd explained. "Even professionals do it." Later, she'd have to ask Molly if she still bracketed after all those years of shooting.

The camera made Lorrie feel brave. Not only was she boldly taking pictures of Thomas, she was getting closer to the horses, too. She was inside the pen and standing near one when it reared up. Normally she would have turned in her tracks and run, but this time she kept the camera to her eye, snapping with a steadiness that seemed to amaze Thomas.

"I didn't know you were a photographer," he said. He sounded impressed.

This embarrassed Lorrie. Did it look like she was showing off? "I'm kind of taking a class. Thanks for cooperating. People usually hate having their picture taken."

"My sister is a wildlife photographer. She practiced on me for years—before she moved on to elephants and lions."

Lorrie laughed.

"So aren't you on summer break? Where's the class?" he asked.

Lorrie had told him a little bit about Molly already, so now she filled him in about the darkroom offer. "It isn't really a class," she confessed. "She's just helping me get started."

"That's great." He whistled softly. "Molly Price. I'd heard she lived in Bethesda somewhere." He pointed to her camera. "So what do you like to shoot?"

No one had ever asked Lorrie that question. "I don't know," she admitted. "I like people shots, I guess. People doing things." She had that in common with Molly.

Thomas was standing close to a horse. It reached around and nuzzled his ear. Lorrie took a step back. "Does your sister really take pictures of lions?"

Thomas pushed the horse's head away. "Yeah, she does. My parents don't understand how both their kids can prefer working with animals to working with people." He started walking toward the barn. Lorrie could hear someone inside singing. It was that kind of morning. "Ready to get started?" Thomas asked.

She felt completely at ease in the barn today. Perhaps it was the camera around her neck, or the fact that last night at the coffeehouse had been so hard and this seemed so easy, but neither the horses nor Thomas was making her nervous this morning.

Maybe that's why the next thing Thomas did caught her completely off guard.

Lorrie had the brush in her hand and was about to start on Niki when Thomas squeezed her shoulder and turned her to face him. Before she could react to the fact that his face was just inches from hers, he slipped his fingers around the camera strap on either side of her bare neck. "I don't think you want to ride with your camera, do you?" he said, still touching her.

"I guess not." Her voice came out all raspy. Okay, now she was nervous. His fingers lingered just a second longer, and then he lifted the camera over her head.

"I'll put this in the office."

"Don't be a jerk," she whispered to herself when he was gone. She ran the brush hard down Niki's back. The horse's head swung around, and her big brown eyes seemed to be laughing at Lorrie. "Yeah, yeah, I know," said Lorrie out loud. And to herself, *Every girl who comes in here probably has a crush on Thomas.*

Then he was back, leading a saddled Bullet over. "Let's skip the ring this time," he said.

Lorrie thought about yesterday's rain. "Do you think it'll be slippery on the trail? Won't it be muddy?"

"No, it will be fine. Besides, there's something I want to show you. I think you'll like it."

The trail was soft but not slick. After ten minutes of walking their horses, Thomas pulled to a stop and Niki came up beside him, so close that Lorrie could have touched Bullet's fine black mane.

Thomas slid easily off his horse and helped Lorrie do the same. They were standing by one of the many little runoff streams that fed into the larger Rock Creek. "Look there," Thomas said, pointing toward the bank on the other side.

All Lorrie could see were trees and weeds.

"Keep looking," he insisted.

Her eyes sorted through the green, finally picking up shades of gray. Planks of wood. Then she found it—the broken remains of a two-story house. Its collapsed roof and most of the walls were covered thickly with kudzu vines. She held her hands up to her face, trying to frame a shot. How could she capture this on film when she'd barely been able to see it from ten feet away? She decided to come back with her camera.

"I remember when this house was standing," said Thomas, "when there was glass in the windows and the front porch was still there. My grandfather knew the people who used to live here."

Lorrie turned to him. "The grandfather who bought Bullet?"

"Right, my father's dad. He used to run the stable."

"Oh." Lorrie considered this. She was sure that Sarah had told her Thomas's parents were physicians over at NIH, the big medical-research center in Bethesda. Apparently Thomas didn't come from a long line of doctors.

He took quick steps down the bank to the stream, his horse following, and then Niki. Lorrie sat down on a dry rock on the bank and listened to the sounds of the water and the horses drinking. It was such a peaceful spot, and she would have ridden right by it had Thomas not pointed it out.

"My grandfather used to come here to paint." He turned around as if looking for something. "I guess the creek bed has changed. It's so steep now, but he used to set up an easel here."

"So, if your dad's father ran the stables, did your dad work here, too?"

Thomas's face broke into a smile. "You don't know my dad," he said, laughing. And then, more soberly, he added, "He never liked to be anywhere near the barns. It was the lowest kind of work to him. Manual labor—that's what he called it. And then he went on to become a surgeon, someone whose entire livelihood depends on working with his hands."

Lorrie laughed. "But you're here now."

"And he hates that. He keeps telling me that he worked hard to keep me from having to muck out stalls and brush down sweaty horses." Thomas reached down and let the cold stream run over his fingers. "He'd prefer I wore a lab coat, not jeans and dirty boots."

Lorrie glanced down at his boots. They looked clean to her. "Sarah says you're a great manager, that everything runs really smoothly here."

Thomas shrugged. "She should have known my grandpa."

They lingered for a little while longer, watching tiny birds fly back and forth through the glassless windows of the house. Lorrie thought about her own dad and all that he wanted and expected of her. One time, years ago, she'd told him that she wanted to own a doughnut store. "A doughnut store?" he'd said in a shocked voice, as if she'd told him she wanted to grow up and rob banks. She tossed a leaf into the fast-moving creek and watched it travel downstream. "So your dad wants you to be a surgeon like him?"

"A brain surgeon," Thomas corrected, frowning slightly.

The leaf snagged on a rock and then turned itself around and around until it was free. "My dad wants me to be a rocket scientist," she joked.

Thomas dropped the reins and took a seat on the end of the flat stone Lorrie was sitting on. "Sounds like they have big plans for us."

Lorrie smiled. "I think so."

"I wonder what my dad is going to say when I tell him I'm going to be a vet."

"Uh-oh. You plan to be a vet and you haven't told them yet?"

"They're still getting over the shock of the college I chose. They had in mind something more Ivy League. But I've decided to tell them this summer, while we're on vacation. I want to start school with the whole thing out in the open."

Lorrie remembered him lifting Kiss's hooves this morning. She could see him being a vet.

He faced her, his blue eyes intent. "Don't get the wrong idea. My parents aren't all bad. It's just this one topic— my life."

Lorrie laughed. "I know what you mean. Exactly." She told him a little bit about her mom and dad. "And then there's Elaine, my stepmother. It's a little strange, this new woman with my father."

Thomas swiped at the hair falling across his forehead, but his eyes never left hers. "I guess that would be," he said.

"But she's okay. Nowhere near as bad as all those wicked stepmothers you hear about in fairy tales."

Niki was restless, so they mounted and continued their conversation on horseback.

After a while, Thomas looked over at her. "You seem pretty comfortable with Niki. How about taking her up to a trot?"

"A trot?" A quick rush of adrenaline shot through Lorrie.

"She looks old, but she likes to move."

Lorrie leaned sideways to peer at the horse's face. "She looks kind of tired to me. Like she just wants to walk today. Right, Niki?"

"She's not tired," Thomas protested, kicking his heels into Bullet's side. "Come on, Niki. Let's show her what you've got."

"I—" Lorrie began, but her mouth swung shut when Niki started to pick up speed. Lorrie hung on and just concentrated on not bouncing off and over the side. She was in good shape from swimming and riding her bike in hilly Clearfield, but her leg muscles weren't used to hugging a horse. "Thomas!" she finally screamed, laughing at the same time. "Please stop!"

Thomas pulled up on Bullet's reins, stopping him abruptly.

Lorrie hadn't seen a thing when Niki was trotting, so she was surprised to find they were right by the barn door.

"You did great," he said, before she had a chance to yell at him. "I think next week we'll move right on to cantering."

"Cantering?" she gasped before she saw he was kidding.

"Okay, not next time, but by the end of the summer, for sure. Who knows? Maybe we'll even have you jumping."

"Don't even joke about that." Lorrie's legs were shaking when she slid off Niki's back. They were still unsteady beneath her when Thomas returned with her camera and slipped it back around her neck.

"I think you're Niki's favorite rider," he said, his soft mouth just inches away.

Lorrie held her breath. Was he going to kiss her?

Then the phone rang and, moments later, someone called out his name.

Afraid to leave the barn with what had to be the goofiest smile in the world on her face, Lorrie hung around in Niki's stall and gave her horse a thorough brushing before regaining enough of her composure to slip out the back door.

ten

Lorrie was still feeling blissful on Monday morning, and it was a good thing, too, because Elaine and Molly picked up arguing right where they'd left off last week.

"Molly," Elaine finally said, sounding exasperated, "how about we do something different today and go out for a drive? Let's take a look at that apartment you're considering." Elaine was desperate. After an hour or so, Molly hadn't made a single decision about anything. All she'd done was peer into the boxes, or hold a book in her hands, look at it a while, and then put her hands back into the pockets of her sweater and stare out across the room.

"I don't need to go for any drive," Molly stated. "I've seen the brochure. It included a picture."

Lorrie was astounded. "You mean you've never been there?"

Molly lifted her chin and glared at her. "Don't you be sticking your nose into this, missy. I can darn well take care of myself."

But Lorrie had to wonder. How could Molly consider moving somewhere she'd never even visited?

Elaine made another attempt. "Just for a drive, Molly," she argued. "It will do you good to get out of here."

But Molly was having none of it.

They struggled through the rest of the morning, ending it with Lorrie and Molly in the kitchen, going through cabinets and pulling out serving dishes and Tupperware that hadn't been used in years, and Elaine upstairs on the office phone, calling auction houses and moving companies.

Lorrie couldn't stop peeking at the clock. All she wanted to do was get into the darkroom, where she had deposited her supplies that morning. She was going to start with the four rolls of film she'd shot over the weekend.

At noon on the dot, Elaine rushed out the door, and Lorrie and Molly were alone. "You'll need to be wearing clothes that you can ruin," Molly directed, shuffling toward the basement steps.

"I am," Lorrie told her. She'd dressed in an old T-shirt and jeans, clothes that the chemicals could splash on.

"I'm not sure how much I remember." Molly grabbed the railing and began her descent.

"You don't need to help me," Lorrie said. She'd brought her books with her and was sure she could do every part of the process. All but one: getting the film off the spools and into the developing canisters in total dark. She realized now that she'd been too ambitious. She should have shot a practice roll that she didn't care about. But it was too late now.

"I'm going to get you started with developing the film," Molly told her. "Then I'll leave you to the printing. It's the developing that is tricky for beginners."

Lorrie was excited. With Molly's assistance, she could be printing by later this afternoon!

The darkroom smelled like chemicals and Spic and Span. Molly took her seat on the tall stool. "I'm assuming by that eager look on your face that you plan on getting as far along as possible today." It took about an hour for Lorrie to get all the trays and chemicals in their proper places, and for Molly to show her how to use the enlarger and the dryer. Then Molly reached into the pocket of her old green sweater and pulled out a thick black marker. "Here," she said, handing it to Lorrie. "Now write down these steps on that big piece of paper I told you to get."

When that was done, they were ready to develop the film. Lorrie checked to see if Molly looked tired, but the old photographer seemed eager and alert. Leaning against the counter, Molly transferred all four rolls into the light-tight developing tanks while Lorrie, off to the side, waited patiently in the dark.

"You remembered," Lorrie told her when the lights were back on.

"Yes, I did. Now you can take it from here. In the meantime, you've got to practice this part so you can do it on your own next time. I've got old rolls of film upstairs. Get them from me before you leave. You can shut your eyes and practice at home. I can't be coming down here every afternoon."

All Lorrie heard was "every afternoon."

Molly watched her run the film through the wash. "You have something special on that film. Am I right?"

Lorrie told her about the shots of Sarah and her sister. And the ones she had of Thomas and the old house.

"That house shot sounds hard to get. And I'm not sure about the lighting in your bathroom studio," Molly said. "But you'll learn. That's why you're here."

When they came to a good stopping point, Lorrie helped Molly up to the daybed for her nap. Once the tired photographer was lying down, Lorrie leaned over and quickly kissed her cheek. "Thank you so much," she whispered, and then hurried off before a surprised Molly could say a thing.

••••••••••••••••••••••

In the darkroom, Lorrie forgot about everything but the work in her hands. She began by making a contact sheet, cutting each long roll of negatives into shorter strips of five or six frames and then arranging the strips on the enlarger. This way she could make a print of the entire roll.

The process of printing captured her like nothing else she'd ever done. It had happened before, sort of, back in her old high school, but this was much better. There, on the school paper, she'd had to share equipment and work around people, including a teacher who always managed to take over and do it himself. But here she was on her own. With Molly's directions posted clearly on the bulletin board in front of her, she didn't need help from anyone.

When the phone rang much later, Lorrie jumped. She hadn't even known the thing worked. Quickly she glanced at the wall clock. It was seven-thirty.

Upstairs, Molly stomped on the floor. Confused for a second, Lorrie wondered what was up. Then she figured it out. The phone was for her.

Her dad was on the line. "Lorrie?"

"Dad, I'm so sorry," Lorrie began. "I didn't realize what time it was. I'm in the darkroom." Lorrie heard her dad chuckle on the other end.

"I'll be home soon," she promised, looking about her. She was at a good place to stop. "Within the hour, I promise."

Lorrie hung up the phone. Normally her dad hated it when she was late and didn't call, like the time she and Sarah had gone to a movie at the mall over Christmas break and didn't call home until after ten. But this time he hadn't sounded mad at all.

. . . .

That night, Lorrie sat cross-legged on her bedroom floor with a stack of shiny prints in her hand. She had butterflies in her stomach.

In the darkroom she'd seen her pictures, but she hadn't really *looked* at them. She'd been so busy getting used to Molly's enlarger, carefully timing each step. Here in her bedroom, it was like seeing them for the first time. She wanted so badly for them to be good.

Slowly, she spread the eight-by-ten-inch prints out in front of her. One by one, she picked them up and studied them. By the time she reached the fourth print, the excitement she'd been feeling all day was gone.

The pictures were bad. There was no doubt about it. The angles were all wrong, and a couple of the shots were blurry. She couldn't even remember what she was trying to do in most of them. Out of the entire bunch—and she had picked what she thought were the best ones—only a few of Sarah and Amy half-pleased her.

Disgusted, she leaned against her bed. Shutting her eyes, she thought of Molly's work. Molly's pictures had a way of imprinting themselves in her memory. The soldier, the girls building the sand castle, the mystery man with his foot in the ham.

Lorrie tried to remember her own shots, the ones she'd looked at seconds ago, but not a single image came to mind. She sat up and went over each print again. A barn, some horses, a riding trail in the woods. Boring. Even the shots of the collapsed house that Thomas had shown her were a total failure. It looked like a picture of weeds.

What had she done wrong? She threw down the prints, and they slid against one another in a messy pile. How did Molly do it? How did she take pictures that *meant* something?

....

But when it came time the next day to ask her, Lorrie was hesitant. Molly had hardly said a word all morning.

They were sitting now on the screened-in side porch. Elaine had gone in to work. Lorrie handed Molly one of the yogurts she'd brought over and opened one for herself.

It was hot today. Lorrie didn't know how Molly could stand to wear that sweater. Lorrie leaned back in the big chair with its wide arms and rocked. She watched the birds at the feeder in the neighbor's side yard. She listened to the sounds of traffic on the beltway a mile or so away and took in the hot smell of the old screens and wood flooring.

A door slammed, and the woman next door came out to her clothesline with a basket of wet laundry. After a few minutes Molly said, "She hangs up her sheets every single day."

Lorrie watched the woman and thought about how she might capture that picture in black and white. The white sheets, the dark pine across the yard, the brick of the house to the side. She lifted her hands and framed it a couple of different ways.

"I can remember my mother hanging wash," Molly continued. She closed her eyes. "The smell of the wet sheets comes back to me so clearly. Homemade soap and hot sun on the grass. I would lie under the sheets and watch them move in the breeze, white cloth against the blue sky."

Her voice trailed off at the end, but Lorrie didn't realize she was going to sleep until she heard the even sound of her breathing, saw her head slumped to the side, resting comfortably against the back of the chair. Lorrie shut her eyes and drifted off, too.

When she woke up, Molly was already awake. Lorrie reached for her soda. It was warm. "How long have we been sleeping?" she asked.

Molly took down her white hair and pinned it back into place. "I don't know. Never could stand to wear a watch."

They rocked in silence for a few moments, slowly waking up.

"Molly," Lorrie began, getting up the nerve to ask something she'd been thinking about since last night. "I was wondering, if you had some time this afternoon, if you might . . ." She hesitated. Molly waited for her to go on. "I mean, I was wondering, if you're not busy with anything else, or going out or anything—"

Molly snorted. "And where would I be going?"

Lorrie tried again, this time getting right to the point. "Those prints I developed yesterday, I was wondering if you could take a look at them."

Molly nodded. "I guess I could."

Lorrie reached down into the backpack at her side. She tried not to let Molly see how nervous she was.

Molly took her time going through the stack. Finally, she handed them back. She hadn't said a thing.

"*Well?*" demanded Lorrie.

"Well what?"

"Well, aren't you going to give me some feedback, tell me what I'm doing wrong?"

Molly frowned at her. "That's not what you asked me. You asked that I take a look. And I did. I looked at each one."

Lorrie opened her mouth and then shut it again. She ran a hand through her short hair. "I guess I just assumed you'd have something to say."

Molly stared at her, reminding Lorrie for an instant of Niki and her long silent stares.

Lorrie flipped through the stack of prints. "This is so frustrating," she whined. "I thought when I was taking the pictures that each one was turning out good—but look at them." She held up a shot of the old house. "I need someone to help me. I need someone to tell me what I am doing wrong so that I can make the necessary corrections."

Molly's head snapped around. "The necessary corrections! What are you talking about? Do you think it's so easy? Just like that?" Molly gave a weak snap of her fingers.

"You used to teach classes at American University, didn't you?"

"That was years ago," Molly said in disgust. "My Lord, *years* ago."

Lorrie didn't give up easily. "Developing film was something you hadn't done for years. But you taught me how to use the darkroom."

"I saw all those books you brought with you! You taught yourself."

Lorrie slid the pictures back into Molly's lap. "Please," she pleaded. "Just show me the three best shots and the three worst shots. I'll take it from there." Then she added, all innocentlike, "I can pay you for lessons."

Molly's mouth opened and closed like a beak. "Save your money. I'm paying your mother to find uses for what I have."

Stepmother, Lorrie corrected automatically inside her head.

When she didn't say anything more and didn't take the

prints back, Molly finally began leafing through them, rearranging them. At last, Molly held up a shot of the barn. "I'm going to ask you some questions. Don't think too much before you answer." She put the picture facedown in her lap. "Now, what did you just see?"

"A barn."

"What was on the edges of the shot?"

Lorrie hadn't a clue. She tried to remember. She needed to see the print again.

Molly took her hands and reframed portions of the photo. Lorrie leaned over and watched her position and reposition her hands. Lorrie began to see how many different shots had been available to her.

Molly picked up another print.

"Now tell me," she said, sounding more energetic than she had all day, "what would you see here if you'd dropped to your knees?"

Dropped to her knees? Lorrie had never even given it a thought.

And so it went. Molly took each print and made Lorrie reconsider where she had stood with her camera and what could have been different. Finally, Molly handed back the pile. "If you want to be good at this, you can't just point and shoot."

"Point and shoot?" She hadn't done that! Lorrie wanted to protest, but she couldn't. Molly was right. For each shot, there had been a hundred possibilities.

Molly put her forefinger down on the print at the top of the stack. It was a close-up of Thomas. He was looking down at the horse's hoof. He was focused. Serene. The more Lorrie looked at this one, the more she liked it, no matter what might be technically wrong with it.

"That boy reminds me of someone," Molly said simply.

Lorrie knew. "The soldier," she said.

Molly looked surprised.

"I know your pictures better than I know my own," Lorrie said.

Molly pondered this and then spoke again, her voice low and serious. "I picked him out the first day in camp," she said, remembering. "He was tossing a football to a buddy of his, and there was just something about him." A small smile broke across her lips. "He was playful. Liked to tease me, flirt a little, even though I was old enough to be his mother." And then, more pensively, "There was something about him that set him apart. He wore his heart on his sleeve, I guess you could say. What he felt inside showed on his face." She drew a gnarled finger over Thomas's eyes. "Like this young man right here."

Lorrie leaned over to get a better look at Thomas. He photographed well. She could see why his sister used him to practice on.

"He was so brave," Molly said, speaking again of the soldier. "Even when he was scared, he was brave. Of course, all of them were scared. But he wasn't ashamed to show it. And for the camera, too."

"He looked peaceful when he died," Lorrie offered.

"Yes."

Lorrie could see his face, a fine spray of blood from his chest wound, or maybe that of a buddy's, across his cheekbones, his sad eyes finding Molly and her camera to say good-bye.

Molly looked off into space and kept talking. "That was the one and only time I quit shooting. After that boy. I'd shot rolls and rolls of the war, all manner of terrible things, but when he died right there before me, it hit me hard.

Afterward, I made sure that his family got all the pictures—every frame—that I took of him. I wasn't sure if that was the right thing to do at the time, but later, much later, they wrote to thank me."

They were quiet for a few minutes. A bird chirped. The woman next door came out with another load of wash.

"I'm tired," Molly said, rising from her chair. "I'm going upstairs to lie down in my bed. All this talking has worn me out."

eleven

"I still can't believe you're working with Molly Price," said Sarah. They were standing together in the shallow end of Lorrie's pool, down on their knees, so that the water was just under their chins.

"Yeah, yeah, yeah," Lorrie said irritably. "You don't need to make such a big deal out of everything."

Sarah gave her a long, puzzled look. "Oh-kay," she said slowly.

They were both silent. Lorrie was angry with Sarah for promising that she'd be over for dinner yesterday and then calling at the last minute to cancel because Joel, who was in a band, was "feeling off" and she needed to be back-stage when he performed. "Feeling off," Lorrie had mut-tered angrily to herself when she slammed down the phone. What was *that* supposed to mean?

Sarah had called back this morning to apologize and ask if she could come by tonight, but things still weren't right between them.

Lorrie scrunched down a little deeper and blew bubbles in the water.

"How did the pictures turn out?" Sarah asked her.

Lorrie shrugged. "They could have been better."

"Can I see them?"

Lorrie's pictures already hung all over Sarah's house, records of dozens of family gatherings. She had never hesitated to share her work with Sarah, but now, for the first time, she was reluctant. "They aren't very good," she muttered.

"Who says?"

"Me." She went underwater and wet her hair back. That was the wrong thing to do. Now she was chilly. "I'm making a lot of mistakes."

Sarah was shivering, too. "Let's go get warm." She lifted herself out of the pool and then turned and offered Lorrie a hand. "Then let's look at your pictures. You know I'm your biggest fan."

Sarah wasn't just trying to be nice. She was impressed with every print. "This is great," she exclaimed, pointing to one of the horse pictures that Lorrie thought was particularly boring. "That's Thunder. I know a little kid who'd love to have a print of this. Thunder is his favorite."

"You can give that to him," Lorrie said. All she could see was the fence railing that cut into the corner of the frame unnecessarily and the way the horse stood dead-center in the shot. But Sarah didn't notice that or any of the other glaring errors. She seemed to like each picture, even the ones of her sister and herself. "My parents are going to love these, Lorrie. These are better than a professional would have done. Really."

"Those aren't the final prints. I'm going to crop them a different way," Lorrie told her, using her hands to frame a shot more tightly. There were still things she could do in the darkroom with this one.

The last print in the stack was the picture of Thomas. Sarah's face broke into a wide smile. "I like this the best," she said in a teasing voice. "How about you?"

Lorrie didn't have to look at the print to know which one her friend was talking about.

"He likes you, you know," Sarah suggested playfully.

Lorrie tried to steer the conversation in another direction. "I like him, too. He's a good teacher."

Sarah wasn't fooled. "You know what I mean. Admit it, Lorrie. He's perfect for you. Smart, good-looking, down-to-earth, fun. Should I go on?"

"No. I'd rather hear about Joel. Do your parents like him?"

Sarah got a stupid grin on her face. "Well, my dad would definitely be happier if he played the violin instead of the guitar, and my mom has all these crazy ideas about musicians and drugs—none of which are true for Joel—but aside from all that, yes, I think they like him." She didn't sound completely convincing. She grabbed a stuffed dragon from the bed and started tossing it up and down. "He's not like the others, Lorrie. I just want to be with him every minute."

"I figured that out." Lorrie knew it was silly, but it hurt her. Sarah had been out with Joel far more than she'd been over here with her this summer.

The stuffed dragon fell out of the air onto the floor. Sarah let it lie there, its goofy face smiling in Lorrie's direction. "I'm sorry, Lorrie. I am so gone on this guy. I can't explain it. It's getting me in trouble. My parents are having a fit. I'm not keeping up around the house, and I've come in after my curfew a couple times."

"I can't believe what they let you get away with."

Sarah picked up the dragon again and petted the felt spikes on its back. "It's funny how we have both hooked up with older guys."

"What?! I'm not hooked up with anybody, Sarah."

Sarah laughed. "Okay, okay, *don't* admit that you're crazy about him."

Lorrie slid her prints under the bed and out of the way and stood up. "Okay, I won't. Now let's do ice cream," she said, jumping off the bed and getting out of the room before Sarah could say anything else.

....

Later that night, after Sarah was asleep, Lorrie sneaked down to the study. Her mom had said to call anytime, and now seemed like the right time. It was midnight here. Nine o'clock on the West Coast.

She hadn't expected to feel so emotional when she heard her mother's voice.

"Lorrie? Oh, sweetheart, is that you?"

It was such a familiar sound that Lorrie wanted to laugh and cry at the same time. First her mom talked and Lorrie listened, just happy to hear her voice. In the few weeks that they'd been apart, her mom had somehow become less real, less animated in Lorrie's mind, just a collection of traits and quirks somehow frozen in time. On the phone with her now, Lorrie's mother was her real self, full of life, calling her "sweetheart" and telling her all about her roommates, her new house, her job search, and her latest craze, a new puppy.

When it was Lorrie's turn to talk, she found herself chatting as if they were in the same room. Lorrie told her about the riding lessons, about Sarah's being over, about the job.

Her mom asked how it was living there, and how she liked Elaine. When they'd exhausted every subject, Lorrie reluctantly closed the conversation by promising to put some of her new prints in the mail. "I'll send you my best ones."

After she hung up, Lorrie sat by the phone for a long time. She remembered being at Sarah's house last year, during the week after her older sister had gone away to college. Sarah had walked around the house crying, not even trying to stop. But a month later, she was okay. "It's a good sad," Sarah had told her. "We miss her, but it's okay. She is happy there, and it would be awful if she hadn't gone to college and had stayed home."

Now she knew what Sarah had meant. This was sad some of the time, yet it was good, too. Lorrie missed her mom, but she liked being here with her dad. She couldn't have them both, and this was as good as it was going to be. Like a zillion other kids in America, she was always going to be missing one of them.

....

Now that Lorrie knew what she was doing wrong with her picture-taking, she was eager to go out and shoot more rolls, this time correcting all the mistakes she'd made on the first ones. On Friday, after working all morning at Molly's, she chose film for the bright, hazy day that she'd be working with and tried to think of somewhere special to go.

Then she thought of the Potomac River. It wasn't too far from her house, and she'd ridden there before. She could go to Great Falls, where the water rushed downstream in torrents. And the C & O Canal towpath was there, too, parallel to the river, with a mule-drawn barge she could take pictures of.

She called her dad and let him run through all the possible dangers of her riding the five miles over there before he agreed to let her go. "Take the cell phone," he instructed. "And pack plenty of water and some granola bars and fruit."

Finally, she had to cut him off. "I'm out of here, Dad. I'll call you later—or you can call me. I'll leave the phone on."

She used to ride all over the countryside in Pennsylvania. Twenty miles a day sometimes, and lots of hills. Except for the traffic, this was nothing.

She reached the river easily and decided to lock her bike by the old stone tavern and walk the rest of the way, so that she could stop and shoot more easily. It was a short walk along the canal to the trail leading over to the falls.

Ten minutes later, she was beginning to realize that being in a good location wasn't everything. Sure, she was paying more attention to what was in each frame, but she knew as she hit the shutter again and again that her shots were just as boring as the last ones. She couldn't imagine Molly being content with pictures of turtles on a log, or ducks begging for bread crumbs. And the shots of the mule pulling the barge were just plain touristy. She wanted her pictures to say something.

She thought about packing up the camera and spending the rest of the afternoon biking. The towpath was two hundred miles long or something. She could go west and pedal into the countryside, toward Cumberland. Or she could go east and end up in Georgetown close to where she'd been the other night with Sarah and her friends.

She walked a little farther and thought about what Molly might do here. Wouldn't a good photographer be able to find shots anywhere? Off the towpath now, she took the wooden walkway to the falls. The air got cooler, and the sound of rushing water told her she was getting close.

She stood on the wooden observation deck, mesmerized by the frothing, violent water hurtling down over the big gray rocks. Virginia was just across the river. She lifted her camera and scanned the scene. She snapped a few shots for her mom, because her mother loved this place, too, but her pictures of the falls had to look like every other waterfall picture that had ever been taken. She wished something like a big tree or a house would come rushing down the river. Or maybe even a dead body, she thought guiltily. People were drowning in this river all the time. Now, *that* would be exciting.

She played around with her camera for a while, working with the shutter speed and aperture to capture the falling water in blurry motion or sharply focused droplets. She jotted down the settings in a little notebook, so she could figure out later what had worked. Then she stood for a long time with her camera hanging around her neck and let the water hypnotize her. The high, thin voice of a little boy at her feet brought her out of her trance.

"Shells," he was saying to his mother. "There's shells all over."

Shells? They were on high ground here. She watched the little boy scratch in the dirt and pick something up.

"See?" he said to her when he saw she was watching.

She leaned over and looked into his dirty hand. He was right. In his palm were several tiny spiral-shaped shells, like miniature snails.

"They're everywhere," he said.

Hundreds of white shells were embedded in the dirt. It would make an interesting shot, Lorrie decided. She was glad she had a macro lens with her. She slipped it on. It would make these minute things look huge. Crouching down, she brought the white spirals in focus against the sandy soil. Why not play with something artsy? she thought, abandoning all hopes of doing anything significant that day.

For the rest of the afternoon, Lorrie stuck with the macro lens, taking extreme close-ups of things she'd walked right by before. Pools of water on the boulders along the path, flowers sticking out of rock crevices, interesting mosses on the sides of trees. There was no point in being so serious that she couldn't have some fun.

twelve

The next morning, Lorrie couldn't wait to see what she'd gotten on film. Trouble was, she'd never asked Molly if she could come on the weekend.

By ten-thirty, she was going crazy. Elaine had gone into work to catch up there, Lorrie's dad was off at one of those battle re-enactments that he liked so much, and Sarah was at the stables. Lorrie was so bored that she cleaned her room, emptied the dishwasher, and vacuumed the pool. Then she decided she was being silly. There was no reason why she couldn't go over to Molly's and ask.

She'd tap lightly on the door. If Molly was right there, say, in the kitchen, Lorrie would just ask her whether it was okay if she worked in the darkroom. If Molly was asleep, she would get back on her bike and ride away.

It turned out that she didn't have to knock at all. Molly was sweeping the front stoop when Lorrie rode up.

That was strange in itself, but weirder still was seeing Molly wearing her nightgown and no robe.

"Molly, what are you doing?" Lorrie asked, hopping off her bike.

"What does it look like I'm doing?"

Lorrie just stood there, taking in the scene. Maybe on weekends Molly stayed in her nightgown until noon. Still, there was something unsettling about her appearance.

"I was wondering—would it be okay if I worked in the darkroom today?" Lorrie asked, deciding that she'd get started only when Molly was back inside.

Molly rambled on about how dirty the porch had been, but that was troublesome, too. Elaine had hosed it off yesterday. The front stoop couldn't have gotten dirty again already.

"Can I make you some tea?" Lorrie asked when they were finally in the kitchen. She took a good look at Molly. Not only was she in her nightgown, but her hair didn't look like it'd been touched since yesterday.

"That would be nice," said Molly, who settled into a chair. "I can't seem to wake up this morning."

Lorrie took her time assembling the tea, talking over her shoulder while she was arranging the cups, setting out cookies, and waiting for the water to boil. Molly's appearance unnerved her, and she kept expecting to be told to stop "chattering like a blue jay." But Molly just stared down at her hands and waited quietly for Lorrie to set the cup in front of her.

It was only when she demanded, "You're not over here to check up on me, are you?" that Lorrie started to relax.

"I can take care of myself," Molly griped. "I told Elaine that I don't like people hovering over me and I meant it."

Lorrie didn't want to anger the old woman, but she didn't want to pretend she wasn't worried, either. When she finally said that finding her out there in her nightgown was disturbing, Molly looked at her for a long moment and then glanced down at herself, seeing, perhaps for the first time, that she hadn't dressed yet today.

"Well, I'll be," she said, sounding a little bit embarrassed. "I wish you'd said something when you rode up. You must think I've lost half my mind!"

Lorrie smiled sheepishly. "Next time, I'll yell at you from the top of the street. Hey, Molly, you're out here in your PJs!"

They both laughed, and Lorrie felt enormously relieved that Molly was okay.

"I took some pictures out at the river yesterday," Lorrie said, munching on a snickerdoodle. She'd love to see how slow-moving Molly managed to make cookies without burning them. "I wanted to print them today, if that's okay. Would I be bothering you?"

"Suit yourself," Molly said, rising from the table. "I'm going to lie down for a while."

Promising herself she would check on Molly in a couple of hours, just to be sure she was really all right, Lorrie skipped down to the darkroom. Already it felt like it belonged to her.

With a whole day ahead of her, she decided to work slowly. First she developed the rolls from the river and made contact sheets. She studied each shot before selecting which frames to print.

She spent hours at the enlarger, experimenting with techniques she'd read about in her photography books. It was fun to try things like dodging and burning in, where she held back or added light to different parts of her prints. She thought about how good she'd be at this craft if only she could spend every day like this one.

Finally, all her work was out of the developing trays and she was at the print dryer, feeding the wet sheets in one by one and chewing on the Snickers bar she'd brought with her. She glanced at the images but didn't really see them. She scribbled a few notes in her darkroom notebook and deposited the dry pictures on a shelf in an empty cabinet. Today's work was strictly practice. She didn't plan to show it to anybody, not even Molly.

Molly! Lorrie had been so caught up that she'd completely forgotten her. Lorrie glanced quickly at the big black clock on the wall. Now that she thought about it, she couldn't recall hearing a sound in the house for the entire day.

She tore up the stairs. "Molly?" she called, trying not to sound as anxious as she felt.

After Lorrie had searched both floors, she couldn't keep the pure panic out of her voice. "Molly? Where are you?" She stood in the doorway of the bedroom. The room was empty. The bed was made. The nightgown that Molly had been wearing that morning hung from a hook on the bathroom door.

The sight of it calmed Lorrie, if only for a moment. At least Molly had managed to get dressed and put her room in order. But where was she now?

Lorrie searched the house again and had the kitchen phone in her hand to call Elaine when she noticed that the door to the backyard was not quite shut. She put the phone down and yanked open the door.

How could Molly possibly be back there? The grass was long and weedy, and the yard was littered with branches and sticks that had fallen over the years.

But once she was outside, Lorrie discovered that the path through the grass wasn't as narrow as it appeared. She hadn't taken more than a few careful steps along it when she caught a glimpse of Molly's green sweater.

The sweater moved. There was Molly, sitting on the wooden bench.

Running now, Lorrie reached her quickly. "Molly, what are you doing out here?" she screamed when she got to her. "I've been looking all over for you. You scared me half to death. First the nightgown and now this!" Ignoring the shocked look on Molly's face, Lorrie ranted on, "You could have tripped on a limb and broken a leg or something. You're lucky I found you when I did."

Molly straightened her back and stuck out her chin. She glared at Lorrie, her little eyes hard with anger. "I do believe, missy," she spat, "that I have the right to sit in my own backyard."

Lorrie glared back. She wasn't ready to give in yet. Her heart was still pounding.

"What do you think I do when you're not around? Just sit and stare at the walls?"

Lorrie was speechless. She was sweating from her frantic house search.

Molly patted the bench. "You are all worked up, aren't you?" she said, her voice suddenly gentle. "Come here. Sit down and calm yourself."

Lorrie plopped down beside Molly. She was nearly in tears. "I've been looking and looking for you! I didn't know where you'd gone."

"I'm sorry to have worried you," Molly said warmly, the anger completely gone. "I come out here sometimes in the evenings."

Lorrie glanced around her. It was a lovely spot, secluded and cool. A high privacy fence separated them from the neighbors, and the huge oak cast this part of the yard in deep shade. She leaned back against the bench and took a few deep breaths. She began to relax.

"You were down there for hours," Molly said, watching as Lorrie stretched her legs out in front of her. "You should pace yourself."

"I lose track of time," Lorrie admitted. Then she told Molly about yesterday's shooting and today's work. "This photography business is harder than I thought it would be."

"Of course it's hard." Molly snorted. "I guess you're used to picking things up quickly," she said, her tone softening. "Elaine told me that you are a good student. Smart."

Lorrie shrugged. "I do okay. But I'm not talking about school. When I take six rolls of film, I expect to get at least one good shot."

"I see."

Lorrie could hear the smile in Molly's voice. "It's not as if I have to do this," Lorrie said defensively.

"You certainly don't."

"There are other things that I do quite well."

Molly chuckled softly. "I'm sure there are. We just went over that."

Lorrie waited for the old photographer to say more, something about the value of persistence and patience and hard work. But Molly was watching a squirrel with its mouth full of leaves scramble up and over the fence.

There wasn't going to be any lecture. This wasn't school.

Moments passed. The sun was beginning to set, although there were hours left of the summer evening. Lorrie wondered if bats came through here at dusk.

After some time, Molly waved a hand at the yard. "This used to be such a showcase," she said.

"A showcase?" repeated Lorrie. "You can't be serious. *This* yard?"

"It most certainly was. You saw the picture by the back door."

Lorrie didn't see anything that could have been in that shot. Only the bench, and Albert Blake standing by it, holding his floppy gardening hat. Lorrie looked about her. Now that Molly mentioned it, there were signs that things had once been different. There in front of them, for instance, was a row of stonework that might have been a garden border. And under the honeysuckle, which was sprawling across the ground and up the wooden fence, were a few choked black-eyed Susans and something else, something made out of stone. Lorrie went over and yanked back the honeysuckle, uncovering a little garden statue. "Look here, Molly," she called over her shoulder. "It's a frog."

"There were flower beds everywhere," Molly explained. "All along the fence rows. Beside paths of crushed stone. Around this tree. Albert even had a fountain back here somewhere, with goldfish in it, I believe." She squinted toward a distant part of the yard. "The underground hose has rotted out by now, but it was a beautiful little spot. Very lovely. The whole backyard was."

"You two must have worked hard on it."

"Us two? Oh, no, I had nothing to do with it. I wasn't even in the country half the time back then. This was Albert's project. The only garden I've ever kept is that neglected one out front. Oh, no, this was Albert's love."

Lorrie cleared around the base of the stone frog. There was nothing in the books about a backyard garden kept up by Albert Blake. She wanted to know more about Molly's relationship with this man, this *married* man. "He must have spent a lot of time here," she said casually. "Days and days, I'd guess, if he had this yard looking like a showcase, as you put it."

"Now, don't you go getting the wrong idea, missy," Molly said sharply, catching Lorrie's hidden question. In what was for Molly a speedy gesture, she pulled herself to her feet.

Lorrie thought that she was heading back in for the night, but instead she stepped across the rock border and reached for a long strand of honeysuckle.

"What are you doing?" Lorrie demanded, grabbing Molly's arm protectively.

"I have the right—"

"I know, I know. You have the right to sit in your own yard. You have the right to pull honeysuckle. You have all kind of rights," she concluded lightly. Gently, but firmly, she steered Molly back to the bench. "Here," she said, "let me entertain you. I've pulled honeysuckle before, and I ended up falling on my butt a couple of times." When she saw that Molly was going to stay put, Lorrie returned to the tenacious weed. "You can sit there and give me orders. I think that might suit you," she said slyly.

"Yes, I think it might," Molly agreed with a smile.

Lorrie yanked at the sweet-smelling vine that had taken over the fence. It felt good to give her body this workout after being bent over an enlarger in the close darkroom all day.

When she'd cleared about three feet of fence, she came back to the bench so the two of them could admire the work together. But when she looked at Molly, she found that her companion had fallen asleep.

. . . .

"It sounds like you really like her," Thomas said the next morning as they were walking their horses along the trail, Niki a body's length behind Bullet.

They came up to the old house by the creek. Lorrie studied it, trying to figure out how to reshoot it. It wouldn't be easy to achieve the effect that she wanted. There was so much vegetation, so much texture, that the prints she'd made were cluttered and confusing. Maybe in the fall, when the leaves were gone, she could get something she liked on film. "If you're interested," she said, turning to look at Thomas, "I could bring over a couple of the books from the library. You could see her work. It's *so* good."

They didn't get off their horses, just talked and rode for the entire hour. Lorrie's body was aching from the gardening she'd done last night, when she'd kept up her attack on the honeysuckle until it got too dark to see. Today's conversation had a laid-back, rambling feel to it.

She felt comfortable and totally at ease with Thomas. To her, this was special, but she didn't know if he felt the same way.

"What I'd like to see is *your* work," Thomas said. "Sarah says you're good."

Lorrie was a lot more comfortable talking about Molly. "I'm a beginner," she said with a shrug.

"Sarah showed me a picture that you took of her dad."

Lorrie knew the shot. She'd snapped it at Sarah's eleventh-birthday party. Anybody else would have stopped carrying it in her wallet years ago.

"I'm interested in your work," he insisted.

Lorrie tried not to let on how much this pleased her. "If I show you my pictures, you have to agree that these are the 'before' shots."

"Before what?"

"Before I get really good at this."

Thomas laughed. "Okay, it's a deal. I get off at two this

Wednesday. Do you want to get together? Maybe meet here and then go out for a late lunch?"

Lorrie nodded in agreement, and they made plans to eat at a nearby deli. She didn't know if this was really a date, but that's certainly what it felt like to her.

The barn was in sight. The path was a clear stretch in front of them.

"Last week was fun, wasn't it, when we took the horses in at a trot?" Thomas caught her eye and waited for her response.

"Oh, no, no way. Not that again—"

"Come on, Lorrie. You saw how happy it made your horse."

"That's not fair, Thomas. You're always using poor Niki." Lorrie laughed, her fingers tightening around the reins.

"Poor Niki nothing. She loves this." He moved his horse forward on the trail and just before kicking him into a trot called back, "Okay, okay, you two old folks can walk, but Bullet and I are going to put a little speed into this ride."

"Thomas! That's—" Lorrie started to protest as she felt Niki increase her pace to catch up with the faster, younger horse.

Lorrie had to make a split-second decision: stop Niki or follow along. Maybe she was just too tired this morning to protest, or maybe she was ready for the risk. She tried to stop thinking and just let herself go along, relaxing into the ride Niki was giving her.

Sarah was in the yard with a student when Lorrie and Thomas rode up, and her grinning face was the first thing Lorrie saw when her horse came to a stop.

Sarah gave them both a thumbs-up and was coming toward Lorrie when Thomas, leading Bullet back into the barn, called over his shoulder, "Good riding, Lorrie. I'll see you Wednesday at two."

Lorrie ignored Sarah's raised eyebrows. "I've gotta go brush down Niki," she said, leaving her friend standing there, dying to know more.

thirteen

Lorrie hurried home, pedaling fast through the parks and side streets of Bethesda. A quick shower and over to Molly's, that was her plan.

But it wasn't her father's. As soon as she came through the front door, he appeared in the kitchen doorway. "Good, you're back. We can get an early start."

"An early start?" she repeated, pulling off her helmet.

"I thought we'd spend the day together. Remember, I asked you last night if you had any plans for today?"

"I didn't mean I was free to *do* something," Lorrie blurted out.

"We're taking a day trip, and we'd like you to join us."

Her groan brought a frown to her father's face. She had to think fast. "Thanks for thinking of me, Dad, but I'm sure you guys would have more fun without me along. You're newlyweds. You must want some time alone."

"Lora," he said firmly, using her given name. "I think you've got this a little bit wrong. Elaine and I have lunch in the city a couple of days a week—or at least we did until just recently—and we go out at night all the time. It's *you* I never spend any time with."

Lorrie set her helmet on the closet shelf and tried to think how to argue her way out of that one.

Her father tapped his watch. "We'd like to leave within the hour, if you can be ready."

"How about a day by the pool instead? I'll clean it and make you guys lunch."

"We'd like to get an early start," he said, ignoring her offer.

Lorrie was halfway up the stairs when she remembered to ask where they were going.

"Point Lookout. It's the site of an old Confederate prison camp."

"Oh, joy," she muttered under her breath.

"Bring your camera," her father called as she reached her bedroom door.

She felt her mood lighten. At least there was that.

....

Point Lookout was south of the city, on the Chesapeake Bay. She'd seen it on the map but had never been there. Riding through the Maryland countryside, Lorrie looked out the window and listened to Elaine and her dad in the front seat. Her dad was a real history buff, that she knew. What she hadn't realized was that Elaine was, too. Then she remembered that they'd met through one of her dad's lecture series at the museum.

Point Lookout was a pretty place, a narrow point of land where the Potomac River fed into the bay. The place had an island feel, kind of desolate and isolated. The prisoners must have hated it here with the cold winds off the water in the winter months. Lorrie had to admit that she liked history, too. The way her dad taught it to her, it was all about people, not facts and dates. And now, while she scrambled around the remains of an old fort where tents had been set up, she could imagine what it must have been like to be held here, imprisoned far from home and freezing to death.

"You might be able to catch ghosts on film," a park guide suggested when she saw Lorrie shooting. "Point Lookout is supposedly haunted, you know." Lorrie's dad had told her stories on the drive down, one about a prisoner spotted running on the road, another about a woman on the beach asking about her husband lost at sea. "Maybe something will show up on your film," the guide told her now.

Lorrie had heard of ghosts appearing as mysterious blurs on film, but she saw nothing through her lens, or on the beach, or near the lighthouse, which was also said to be haunted. Even so, the ghost stories gave her a creepy feeling that she liked.

She took a shot or two of the water and the beach, but mostly she looked for people. People doing things. Kids on the pier, learning to fish, or families on the docks, dangling strings loaded with pieces of chicken and then pulling up blue crabs that they dropped into bushel baskets to cook for dinner.

Lorrie wrote down names and addresses in her little notebook and promised to mail prints. "It'll be in black and white," she told them. "I'm taking a class." She still liked to think of it that way, that Molly was giving her private lessons. She didn't tell them this, or that her teacher was Molly Price.

All day she thought about that morning's promise to Thomas. What work would she show him? What could she possibly have ready by Wednesday at two?

On the way back home, they stopped for an early dinner at Solomons Island, a little town on the Chesapeake Bay. The three of them ordered crab cakes and sat at a table near the water, where they could watch boats coming into the busy harbor. They talked of other places to go in Maryland and Virginia, and Lorrie found that another day trip with her dad and stepmom didn't sound all that bad. Her dad was a different guy around Elaine, relaxed and happy. It was no longer Lorrie's job to keep the peace.

....

When the telephone woke her, Lorrie thought it was morning, but it wasn't quite. It was four-thirteen. Lorrie leapt out of bed, and then the phone stopped ringing. She heard Elaine talking.

Lorrie immediately thought of her mother. *Maybe Mom's been in a car accident.* She went and stood by the doorway of her dad and Elaine's room.

Elaine waved her in. "No, I don't know what medication she's on," she was saying.

Something had happened to Molly.

"It's written down, taped to the kitchen cabinet," Elaine continued. She listened for a couple of minutes. "I'll be right there." She hung up the phone.

Lorrie couldn't bear it. "Is she okay?"

Elaine stood up and ran a hand through her hair. "I think so. Apparently Molly passed out in the upstairs hallway. When she came to, she managed to crawl into her office and call for an ambulance. They are running some tests." Elaine gave them a tight smile. "She's being so difficult and giving everyone such a hard time that it sounds like she must be okay. I could hear her in the background, barking at someone. I'm going to stop by her house on the way over. They want to take a look at her medications."

Lorrie's dad opened the closet door. "I'll go with you."

"I'm fine, really. There's no need. You know how hospitals are. Everything takes forever."

He pulled a shirt off a hanger. "It's the middle of the night. I'll run you over to Molly's, and then you can drop me back off."

"Roger—"

"I'll feel better, Elaine. It's not even light yet."

Lorrie finally found her voice. "I'll come." She hated hospitals more than anything, but she should be the one to go.

Elaine gave her a quick hug on her way to the bathroom. "You guys are wonderful. Okay, Roger, you can come along, if you'd like. Lorrie, it'd be a big help to me if you could be at Molly's this morning. Natalie Dunn is in Europe, but we have a telephone appointment set up for ten o'clock. Molly was supposed to have signed some papers that I left on her desk. Dr. Dunn might ask about those. If you could just take that call and explain the circumstances, I'd really appreciate it."

"No problem."

"Thanks. I'll have my cell on if you need anything."

While the two of them got dressed, Lorrie made coffee and toast and left it out for them in the kitchen. Then she crawled back into bed and waited for it to be morning. Falling back to sleep was out of the question. Her mind kept reviewing yesterday—or was it the day before?— when she spent the day at Molly's. She had been so strange that morning, out there sweeping the porch in her nightgown. Why hadn't she told Elaine, so they could check on her before taking off on their trip? It would have only taken a minute.

....

Not long after she spoke with Natalie Dunn, Lorrie heard the car pull into the driveway. She ran down to the front window in time to see Elaine help Molly from the car. When she'd called from the hospital, Elaine had said that Molly needed her prescriptions adjusted and was "just a little bit tired," but as soon as Lorrie saw her friend, she knew that Molly was more than a little tired. She was wiped out.

Lorrie tried not to cry. Molly looked like she was a hundred and fifty years old. She was leaning heavily against Elaine, and she could barely lift her slippered feet to step across the yard to the front door. Running out to help, Lorrie wondered why Elaine hadn't thought to get a wheelchair. They didn't even attempt to get her to her bedroom. The daybed would be fine until she got her strength back.

Lorrie thought Molly would be asleep before she returned with the tea that Elaine suggested she make, but her eyes opened when Lorrie entered the room.

Gratefully, Molly took the cup and held it steady while she took her first sip. Her glance fell on Lorrie, and there was no mistaking the affection on her face. "Thank you, dear," she said.

The gentleness in her voice brought tears back to Lorrie's eyes. Not wanting Molly to see them, she busied herself with her tea, adding sugar and cream and tasting it several times before she felt she could turn back around.

Elaine reached into her bag for her car keys. "I'm going to run out and fill these prescriptions before we get started."

"Get started?" Lorrie couldn't believe she'd heard right. "We're going to work today?" She looked back to Molly, whose eyes were slowly shutting.

Elaine shot Lorrie a glance. "We had a chance to talk at the hospital. We decided to shift things around a bit and have you start on some interior work. That'll give Molly a break from sorting, and I can get caught up with the legal stuff. I've gotten a little behind." She took a seat next to the daybed. "Molly, would it disturb you if Lorrie began prepping the kitchen today?"

Molly's head moved back and forth, just barely. Her eyes stayed shut.

Elaine took Molly's cup from her hand and motioned for Lorrie to follow her out of the room.

In the kitchen, Elaine whispered, "I was hoping to put this off until Molly moved out, but it might work out if we do a little painting now. Or at least if we *prepare* to paint."

Lorrie nodded in agreement. Molly had had it with going through boxes for hours at a time.

Elaine glanced at her watch. "I've got to be in court later today. Could you possibly hang around, get started in this room, and maybe work on your photography this afternoon?" She sounded exhausted.

Lorrie was surprised that Elaine would hesitate to ask. "No problem. I can sit with her—"

"No, don't sit with her. We had a big argument at the hospital about that. I wanted to bring in a nurse. I wanted to get a wheelchair. Oh, you should have heard her."

Lorrie smiled. She could imagine.

Keeping her voice low, Elaine continued, "If you'll just check on her every so often."

"Don't worry. I'll call you if anything comes up, or I'll call my dad."

Elaine shot her a grateful look. "Okay, thanks. Oh, and you spoke with Natalie Dunn this morning? You told her about Molly?"

"Yes. She wants you to e-mail her and let her know how Molly is doing. She sounded nice."

"She is. And patient." Elaine took a little notebook out of her shoulder bag. "I've got so much going on right now that I have to write everything down," she admitted. "Okay, now let's figure out how to get started," she said, still writing. "Have you ever done this kind of work before?" She glanced up at the kitchen walls.

Lorrie had painted lots of rooms with her mom. "Oh, yeah. I'm practically a professional," she said with a grin. "I'll start by taking down the pictures and spackling holes." She looked up at the ceiling. "Maybe scrub the dirty spots."

"Wonderful," Elaine sighed. "You are a treasure," she said, kissing Lorrie's cheek. "You'll find spackle and sandpaper in a box at the foot of the basement stairs."

fourteen

After a small lunch with Molly, Lorrie retreated to the darkroom. She laid out her work, marking pictures she might want to show to Thomas.

She didn't forget Molly. Not this time. She kept the process simple, so that there were stopping points at least every hour. Sometimes Molly was asleep. Sometimes she was reading or listening to the radio beside the daybed. Around three, they had tea together, and then Lorrie returned to the darkroom.

She felt relieved. Elaine had laid out all Molly's medicines and given her a little dispenser to keep it all straight. Everything seemed to be fine.

Lorrie had her last print in the wash when she heard a tap at the darkroom door. Startled, she called out, "Molly?"

"It's me, Lorrie. I'm back."

Lorrie let out a deep breath. "Elaine! You scared me. You can come on in. I'm just about through."

Elaine opened the door.

"You can turn on the light."

Elaine flipped the switch. "Oh my. What a wonderful darkroom," she said, glancing around the room. "I'm really impressed."

"I've been checking on her all day."

"I know. She told me. I'm just letting you know I'm here. You don't have to stop. I'm making Molly some soup, and I picked up a sub for you." She took a final look around the room, seeing some early prints Lorrie had tacked to her bulletin board. "Very nice work."

With Elaine upstairs, Lorrie decided to use the time to clean up. Then she looked over the day's images. She had a good shot of Elaine and her dad that she'd caught with a long lens when the two of them were walking on the beach at Point Lookout. She'd cropped it several different ways and enlarged it, and now she chose the print she liked best and slid it into an envelope. She'd give it to them tonight.

When Lorrie got upstairs, she was surprised to find that Molly had made her way up to her office on the second floor. Elaine handed Lorrie a plate with a thick sub on it.

"Thank you." She picked up one of the halves and took a big bite. She smiled at Molly, who was sitting behind her desk. "You look much better," she observed, taking the window seat.

"I'm fine," Molly snarled. "I don't need you two fussing over me."

Happily, Lorrie bit into her sandwich again. "You sure *sound* fine," she joked. She was almost finished with her sub before she realized that something was up. Neither Molly nor Elaine was doing much talking, and Elaine had her yellow legal pad out in front of her.

Before Lorrie could ask, Molly stood up. "I know it's early, but I'm going to bed. I think I'll read for a while and then get some sleep," she said. Elaine followed her out of the room. Lorrie drank her soda and looked out the window. She could see her little pile of honeysuckle and the stone frog.

When Elaine returned and shut the door behind her, Lorrie asked, "What's up?"

Elaine got right to the point. "I got a long e-mail from Natalie Dunn this afternoon." She sounded serious. "She mentioned something that I've been thinking about all day. I had told her about you and how you've been spending a lot of time with Molly."

Lorrie was puzzled. "Yeah?"

"Just think about this before you say anything."

"What?"

"Let me back up a little bit. After today's scare, Natalie feels even more strongly that much will be lost if Molly doesn't talk to someone—"

Lorrie sat very still. She could hear the bubbles popping in her soda can.

"Natalie was impressed with how Molly talks to you so much, how she tells you stories that she tells no one else. She has since that first day in the living room when you told her you thought the sofa was ugly."

"And?"

"Natalie suggested that *you* might start conducting some informal interviews with Molly. That you could, perhaps, set up a tape recorder and ask her some questions. Natalie would work with you, providing you with background information, helping you with the questions, suggesting techniques that might make the interviews go more smoothly."

"More smoothly. . . ." Lorrie couldn't believe she was hearing this.

"Yes. She'd teach you how to adjust the mikes, run the

tape recorder, that sort of thing. She mentioned cameras, but we both thought that was out."

"Cameras? Mikes?"

"Yes. She'd like for this to be a part of the archive."

"Archive?" Lorrie couldn't seem to stop parroting Elaine's words.

"Would you be willing to consider this?"

"Um, well, I . . . ," Lorrie stuttered. "What does Molly say?"

Elaine shrugged. "I haven't really said too much. I hinted around at the idea that Professor Dunn wanted to move on this, arrange an interview. . . . And then Molly clammed up. You came into the room right after."

"She's had a big day."

"I know. But she asked about those papers she'd signed, and it kind of went from there."

Lorrie thought about all that Elaine had just said. "I think we're doing enough right now, without this, too." She felt protective of Molly.

Elaine picked up the tea tray she'd brought up earlier.

Lorrie started to feel annoyed. "I mean, jeez, Elaine, Molly goes to the hospital and suddenly you want to start taping her talking, like she's about to die or something. All this is about her dying, isn't it?"

"Oh, Lorrie, I wouldn't put it that way," Elaine protested. "It's an oral history. People do this all the time."

"No one mentioned it last week."

"You're right. No one did." Elaine slipped her briefcase strap over her shoulder and turned off the desk light. "I appreciate your honesty, and you're probably right. Today is a bad day to discuss this."

Lorrie drank the last of her soda and was quiet.

At the doorway, Elaine turned to her. "Let's go. I'll drop you at home, and then I'm coming back. Before we left the hospital, I made Molly agree to let me sleep here tonight." She saw Lorrie's surprised look. "As you can imagine, she put up quite a fight."

"Oh, I'm sure she did," Lorrie said, shaking her head as they left the house.

At home, she handed her dad the print and tried to escape to her bedroom. But he couldn't stop going on about how great it was, and for the first time in her life, Lorrie questioned his praise. She knew the shot was okay, but it wasn't as good as he acted like it was. It wasn't perfect. There were things about it that were still wrong.

That night in bed, even though she was exhausted from the long day, Lorrie couldn't sleep. She was thinking about Elaine and Natalie Dunn's proposal. One minute, she thought the whole thing sounded kind of fun. She loved hearing Molly talk, and she had plenty of questions that she wanted to ask her. In fact, she already had fifty pages of Molly's stories written down in her computer file. But then, the next minute, Lorrie would roll over in bed and see the stack of books sitting in a pile on her dresser and realize that this wasn't like homework for school. This was a job for an adult, an adult with a degree or something. She hadn't even made it through high school yet. She didn't even drive. The thought of working with a college professor on a project this big was scary.

At one o'clock, she headed to the kitchen for cereal. Just suppose she did agree? What if she botched the whole thing? She ate the cereal dry, out of the box. She hated when she messed up at things. She hated failure.

Rinsing her hands, she looked out over the lit pool. It

was more complicated than that. Lorrie didn't just hate failure: She didn't *do* failure. All her life, she'd been very careful to stick with things she was good at, things where success was easily achieved. Failure was for other people, not her.

fifteen

For the next couple of weeks, Lorrie worked alone a good part of each morning. Elaine's last day at the law firm shifted as she tried to tie up loose ends at the office. It was just as well. Molly was tired and needed a slow pace.

Lorrie liked working by herself, prepping first the kitchen, and then moving into the hallway and front foyer. She enjoyed the rhythm of the work. Sometimes Molly sat and watched her, despite the mess. She seemed happy to see work being done on her house. Much of the time she rested upstairs while Lorrie listened to music and patched and sanded the walls.

In the afternoons, she retreated to the darkroom, stopping periodically to check on Molly. She was working more selectively now, preparing shots to show to Thomas. She'd had to cancel for that Wednesday, but they'd agreed to get together as soon as they could.

In the late afternoons and sometimes the early evenings, she and Molly went to the backyard, where Lorrie pulled weeds and Molly alternated between snoozing and reminiscing.

Lorrie didn't mention Elaine's idea about the interviews, but she sometimes thought, during the long days, that, given the way Molly talked to her so freely, a more formal interview might not be so hard. Lorrie even began asking more questions, pretending sometimes that a tape recorder was getting it all down.

"What's the earliest memory you have?" she asked one afternoon in the garden.

Molly pulled her sweater tight around her and appeared to be thinking about it. "It was when my sister died. I was five. I remember her coffin. It was the tiniest thing."

Lorrie froze, her fingers tight on the trailing vine of honeysuckle.

Without realizing how much this was upsetting Lorrie, Molly continued. "It was probably crib death, though we didn't call it that. My mother found her one morning, and I can still remember the sounds of her screams. She screamed for the longest time. She didn't even know she was doing it until my father came in and made her stop."

Lorrie didn't know what to do or say. She dropped the vine and sat down next to Molly. Neither of them spoke.

Lorrie considered what she would have needed to do if the tape had been running, and suddenly being the one to interview Molly seemed impossible all over again.

....

With all this hard work at Molly's, Lorrie needed downtime at the end of the day. She needed to laugh and play and be fifteen.

She had moved back thinking that even if she and Sarah had jobs they would still have time together, but Sarah was rarely around. Well, she was *around*. She was at the stables. She was out with Joel. She was just not with Lorrie.

In a way, Lorrie had missed her friend less when she was living in Pennsylvania. At least then they'd exchanged letters and e-mail. Now they played telephone tag. Sarah worked all day at the stables and then was out right up to her curfew every night. Lorrie wondered how Sarah, who loved to sleep, was getting by on this schedule.

So did Sarah's mom. Once when Lorrie rode her bike over just to see if she could catch Sarah at home and say hi to the rest of the family, Sarah's mom talked to her for an hour. She wanted to know if Lorrie thought her friend was okay, and if Lorrie knew anything more about this boy, Joel.

Lorrie reassured her that everything was fine, but there were times this summer when she wasn't so sure herself. Sarah was different. It wasn't just her clothes, like her mother suggested. Sarah had always been a little bit crazy in that department, so the low-slung jeans and cropped tops and, most recently, the bright-green streak in her hair weren't so far-out. What *had* changed were Sarah's moods. She seemed uncharacteristically discontent.

"She's probably sleep-deprived," Lorrie reassured Sarah's mom. But Lorrie, too, wondered about Joel. Until now, Sarah's world had been the marching band, field hockey, and school plays. Joel was introducing her to a whole new life, the world of a professional musician who was striving to book performances all over town and to record a CD. He was a senior in high school, but not theirs. It was some alternative school over by the river.

Most of the time, Lorrie buried these concerns. All she really knew was that she missed her friend. There was so much Lorrie wanted to share with her. She wanted to tell her about Molly going to the hospital, about Elaine's suggestion that Lorrie do the interviews for Natalie Dunn. But Sarah had a moment here and ten minutes there. It wasn't enough.

....

On Friday night, after a couple of long weeks at Molly's, Lorrie went down to the stables and found Thomas. She didn't know if he was free, but she was bored and lonely and thought it was worth a try. In her backpack, she had six prints. They weren't perfect, but they were shots she liked.

Thomas was in the office, hanging up the phone, when she entered.

Lorrie felt a deep thrill at the happy grin that broke across his face when he saw her.

"Well, hi. I'm surprised to see you here," he said, coming over to her. "Sarah left about ten minutes ago." He leaned against the front of the desk. Lorrie joined him, not touching his side, but close. It was getting dark outside. The riders were gone; the horses were in the barn. She felt comfortable here with him like this.

"I didn't come to see Sarah," she said shyly.

He gave her a long look—curious, expectant. Just the corners of his lips turned up in a smile. "You came to see me?"

She gestured toward the backpack slung across her shoulder. "I was sorry to cancel lunch, and you wanted to see my work, so I thought . . ." Her voice faded, and her cheeks grew warm. Why had she thought this was a good idea? It was Friday night. Maybe he had a date.

He touched her then, not on purpose but almost. He was reaching behind her to flip on the answering machine, but to Lorrie it felt like an embrace.

"I'm glad you came," he said simply. The machine rewound but he didn't drop his arm. "I'm starving. Do you want to go over to the deli and get something to eat?"

With his arm behind her, grazing her T-shirt right below her shoulder blade, she could only nod in agreement.

"Great." He stood. "Let's lock up." He closed the office window and gestured with his head to follow while he secured the barn for the night. "So you've got some pictures. How many did you bring?"

"Six."

"Six?"

"Yeah, six prints."

Thomas's loud laugh had several of the horses turning their heads. "That's all? You only brought six pictures?"

Lorrie nodded. She could hear him chuckling when he went into the office bathroom to wash up and change his shirt.

Judging from her diminishing paper supply, Lorrie figured she'd probably printed over a hundred shots this summer. Six really wasn't very many, she realized, smiling herself, when Thomas emerged, dressed in clean jeans and a yellow polo shirt. He looked different. Older, attractive.

This was starting to seem like a date.

They tossed Lorrie's bike into the trunk of Thomas's car. It was completely dark now, and the front seat felt small and strangely intimate—not like being in the stables with people everywhere or out on the open trail. Lorrie felt herself get quiet. But Thomas didn't seem to be affected by this new environment. As he drove the short distance to the deli, he talked easily about the neighborhood, telling her about the deep woods that used to be standing where houses were now.

In the restaurant, in a cozy booth, Lorrie began to relax. It was comfortable here, noisy, with dishes clanging and people talking, and the smell of corned beef and pickles in the air. It was a good place to be with Thomas.

After they ordered, she handed him her pictures. And much like Molly had done, he flipped through them, saying little, lingering for a moment or two on each one.

Lorrie swirled her ice cubes with her straw and waited. There were only six prints, but she'd chosen them deliberately. She'd decided to show him the shot of her dad and Elaine from Point Lookout, two of Molly, one of Sarah in the pool, another of the boy at Great Falls, and then, finally, the picture she'd taken of him. He laughed when he saw it.

"They're good," he said sincerely.

She tried to hide her broad smile. "You think?"

"Yeah, I do." He flipped through the pictures again. "I like the way you get people just being themselves. There's an honesty there." He left one of the shots of Molly on top and positioned it so that they both could see it.

It was a picture of her in the darkroom, on her stool, turning to Lorrie with a scowl on her face. Lorrie had snapped the shot quickly, but Molly hadn't protested.

"She looks so frail," Thomas said.

"Do you think so?" Lorrie tried to see her as Thomas did. She loved this image. She had a copy of it in her room at home. It reminded her of that first morning when Molly had opened the door and barked at her and Elaine. Lorrie had been so intimidated in the beginning. Not anymore.

She studied Molly's small, rounded shoulders and the wrinkles around her bright eyes. "She is fragile," she agreed, "though usually I forget that. I guess because she's so sharp and quick in her mind. She never rambles or wanders off in conversation."

They talked about the middle-of-the-night scare, and about the work Lorrie was doing there on the house, and, finally, about Natalie Dunn's offer.

An hour later, the remains of her roast-beef sandwich on the plate before her, Lorrie realized that for the entire meal they'd been talking about her. "So tell me about your fall schedule," she said, turning the conversation to him. "Sarah told me you registered this week."

They stayed for a long time, drinking sweetened tea, sharing a piece of cheesecake, making a last trip to the pickle bar before it closed for the evening. Around them, the dining room slowly emptied out. "We should go," Thomas said finally, standing up and taking her hand to pull her out of the booth.

135

Lorrie was glad she had come to the stables tonight and found Thomas. She had lots of friends in Clearfield, and she missed this kind of thing, going to eat somewhere and hanging out for hours. She was telling him this when they pulled up to her house.

Her dad and Elaine tooted the horn behind them, returning home from a late dinner themselves. Thomas got out of the car, and Lorrie introduced him. After a few minutes of talking about her and her riding lessons, he left. If it had felt like a date, it sure didn't end like one.

sixteen

The next morning, even though it was Saturday, Lorrie went to Molly's and put in a good morning's work pulling wallpaper off the dining-room wall. She enjoyed this kind of thing. Like the honeysuckle project, it was physical and she could see results right away.

She couldn't remember ever finding Molly in such a foul mood before. Maybe it was the humidity: Thunderstorms were forecast. Or maybe it was the work in the house that was unsettling for her. Lorrie heard her climb the stairs three times. It would be best, she knew, just to leave her alone, but last night Lorrie had made a decision. She wanted something from Molly.

After lunch, she had Molly's undivided attention. They were sitting on the side porch. Lorrie had tried to talk her into staying inside, out of the heat, but she wouldn't hear of it.

Her prints were in the backpack in her lap, but Lorrie didn't know how to begin. She played with the zipper, running it back and forth, back and forth.

"Lorrie, will you please stop that?" Molly demanded, batting a hand at her. "What has got you so fidgety today?"

Lorrie took a deep breath, pulled out her stack of prints, and shoved them at Molly. "Can you tell me what you think of these?"

She wished the old photographer looked more pleased. Instead, she was scowling as she went through them slowly, one by one. When she started to hand them back, Lorrie protested. "Wait! What do you *think* of them?"

Molly wrinkled up her nose. "What do you think? What do you think?" she mimicked. "Why are you always asking me that?"

The words stung. "That was mean," Lorrie said in a quiet voice.

Molly pushed the stack back at her. "I can't be telling you everything."

"If you wanted to, you could."

"Well, maybe I don't want to."

Okay, that was enough. Lorrie grabbed her prints. "I'm out of here," she said, crossing the room. Her hand on the doorknob, she looked back. There was something in the way Molly was sitting just then that reminded her of Thomas's observation. Molly *did* seem fragile and frail. "Don't stay out here too long," she felt compelled to say. "It's not good for you."

She waited for Molly to respond, to argue about being able to take care of herself, but the expression on the old woman's face had softened.

"I'm sorry." Molly whispered the words.

Lorrie stood with one foot in the house, the other foot out.

"I was being unkind," Molly said a little louder. "Please come back."

Lorrie stood there for a moment longer, trying to figure out how to handle this. She wished Elaine were around. Then she sat back down sulkily and turned her head away.

"I'm just a grouch today," Molly said. "I don't know why. Please let me see the prints once more."

It would have been easy to be childish here, to pout and say no and make Molly ask again, but Lorrie didn't want to do it that way. She placed the pictures in Molly's outstretched hand. "I thought this bunch was better than the last," she said, sounding more plaintive than she'd intended.

"Yes, I think so, too," Molly agreed.

Lorrie's heart lifted.

Molly flipped through the first few prints. "What do you think makes them better?"

Lorrie didn't understand.

Molly held a print between them. "You do the talking. You'll learn more that way. Now, tell me what you see. Tell me everything you see in the frame, and what you think works here."

"Oh-kay," Lorrie said slowly. It wasn't how she'd envisioned this going. She began describing every little detail in the shot, deliberately exaggerating to release some of the tension she was feeling. "There's a twig there on the ground, beside two small leaves and a chunk of dirt that's the size of a pea. There's a woman wearing a short-sleeved shirt over to the right, fuzzy in the background. And a bird in the sky, that speck there next to a cloud that's shaped like the letter Q." She expected Molly to stop her, to tell her that she was being impertinent, but she didn't seem to be bothered. She nodded her head like one of those shaky-head dogs that people stick on the ledge behind the back seat of their cars. Nodding and nodding, as if Lorrie was doing precisely what she wanted her to do.

They continued like this for a while, Lorrie chronicling every teeny, tiny thing captured in the print. By the fourth shot, something odd began to happen. She was seeing things in the picture that she'd never even noticed before! And this print, this single print, was one she'd literally spent hours on in the darkroom.

Something else was happening, too. As she talked, she saw mistakes she'd made. Like how she'd caught half of a bird in the frame unintentionally, or included one foot but not the other of the little boy.

Lorrie thought that once Molly saw that she'd gotten the point they could stop. But she just kept nodding, and together they went through every single print in the stack. Molly didn't utter a single word until they were done. Then she gripped the arms of her chair, preparing to push herself up, and said, "You're right. It's too hot to be out here."

Lorrie had forgotten all about the heat. "Wait," she cried. "Don't go yet."

"Now what?" Molly sounded like her old cranky self again.

"I was wondering . . ." She hesitated under the force of Molly's glare. "I was wondering," she began again, "if you could maybe tell me what to do. You know, give me some assignments."

"Assignments?"

"Right, like a teacher would. You know. You were a teacher once."

"I can't do that."

"Molly, I've seen your teaching notebooks upstairs."

Lorrie fanned her face with the prints in her hand. "You must know some shortcuts."

"Shortcuts!" Molly hissed. "Professionals don't go looking for shortcuts."

"I'm not a professional. I'm just a kid." It was a convenient excuse, and not one Lorrie was above using on occasion.

Molly was out of her chair and moving slowly toward the door. Lorrie took her silence as an encouraging sign. She knew her friend well enough by now to know that when she wasn't talking she was thinking. And sure enough, when the two of them got to the foot of the stairs, Molly turned to her and said, "Make me a cup of tea and meet me in my office."

Excited now, Lorrie did as she was told and carried the tray up to the sunny workroom. Molly was writing on a pad of paper in that squiggly, old-lady handwriting of hers. Lorrie handed her a cup of tea and was given the paper in exchange. "This should take you a couple of weeks," Molly instructed. "Now, read it out loud and ask me anything you don't understand, because I don't want you pestering me with questions. This work is to be done independently. I've written down the due date as well."

Lorrie read it out loud, asked a question or two, and thanked Molly a whole bunch of times.

"You know why I'm doing this, don't you?" Molly asked, with a look on her face that took Lorrie a moment to recognize. Molly was looking mischievous.

"Uh, to keep me out of your hair for a while?"

"Yes, and for another reason, too."

Lorrie couldn't think what that might be.

"Now, don't let this go to your head, missy. But I think you're a young photographer who just might have potential."

Lorrie didn't even try to hide the grin that spread across her face. *Potential. Molly Price thinks I might have potential.*

Molly was shuffling out from behind her desk. "I'm off to take my nap. Shut that door tight on your way out. I'm spending a fortune on this blooming air-conditioning."

Lorrie smiled and laughed at everything for the rest of the day. "Potential." She'd heard that word a million times. Teachers loved to use it. But this was the first time it really meant something to her. *Molly says that I have potential.*

She wanted to tell someone. She called her mom but got the answering machine instead. She thought about calling her dad, but, as much as she loved him, she knew he would ruin the whole thing. He had, after all, been talking about her potential her whole life.

She thought about paging Sarah, but Sarah was at work, and it might be an hour or two before she could use a phone. So she got on her bike and rode to the stables, hoping to catch her on a break.

. . . .

Lorrie found her friend unloading hay from a truck. It was uncomfortable, itchy work in weather like this, and Sarah was thrilled to see Lorrie. "If you help me," she said, before Lorrie even had a chance to offer, "it'll give me an extra few minutes on my break, and we can spend it together."

Lorrie didn't mind. While they worked, she found herself looking about for Thomas. Whenever anybody approached them, she stopped and glanced around.

Finally, Sarah said, "Lorrie, he's not here. He had to go see one of our suppliers. Something about some questionable feed."

Lorrie didn't pretend she hadn't been looking for him.

She just grabbed another bale and kept her face averted. She hadn't meant to be so obvious.

When the truck was empty, they washed off the pieces of hay and the stickiness from their faces and arms and then cut across the field to an empty picnic table in the shade by the creek.

Climbing on top of the table, Sarah opened a bag of chips and handed Lorrie one of the sodas she'd brought along. "So—what's up? You never come here. Or were you here to see Thomas and you ran into me?"

"I came to see you," Lorrie said, not wanting to respond to Sarah's teasing. "What are you doing later? Do you want to do something?"

"Joel's picking me up and we're going down to Virginia for a gig. I can't wait to get out of here." She brushed some hay off her shirt. "Sometimes I have to ask Joel if I smell like a barn."

"Gig." The word sounded funny coming out of Sarah's mouth, but Lorrie didn't say anything. And Sarah had never been anxious to get away from the stables before. Lorrie thought about how Sarah's mom was so worried about her.

"I came to tell you about something that happened to me at Molly's," she admitted finally. And then she told her friend what Molly had said. It wasn't bragging to tell Sarah.

Sarah had just the response Lorrie was counting on. She jumped off the table and pulled Lorrie off as well to give her a jumping-up-and-down hug.

When they were both sitting again, Sarah said, "Wow! And this from Molly Price. Now maybe you'll believe me. I've been telling you for years, you know."

Lorrie was so glad she'd come here. This was the Sarah she'd been missing. She told her about the four assignments Molly had given her. "They don't sound all that hard," Lorrie concluded.

"You don't think so?" Sarah seemed to consider this. "The one about the textures and the one about the shapes—*those* sound easy. But the assignment where you have to tell a story—that's probably hard, and I don't even know what it means to capture an emotion."

"A single dominant emotion," Lorrie corrected.

"Right."

They talked about it some more, Sarah suggesting places to go. They were lying across the top of the table, faces toward the sky. Sarah was talking, wistfully now. "You guys—you and Joel—you are so lucky. You're artists. You're producing stuff."

"Artists! What are you talking about?"

"Joel's working on a CD. You're a photographer," Sarah said unhappily. "I'm pitching hay and walking kids around a ring on big, dumb horses."

"But you love horses," Lorrie protested. "You even have that bumper sticker on your parents' car. 'Horse people are stable people.'"

Sarah shook her head. "Lorrie," she said, "I am bored out of my mind."

Lorrie didn't know what to say. Horses had never bored Sarah. In fact, Lorrie had never heard her say she was bored with anything.

"Oh well," Sarah sighed. "Maybe I'll feel better after vacation." She was going down to the beach in North Carolina with her parents and her aunt's family. They went every year.

"You don't sound too excited," Lorrie said.

"I want Joel to come, but my parents said no."

Lorrie was glad they were looking up, not at each other. That way Sarah couldn't see how much it hurt that Sarah hadn't invited her. At last, she managed to say, "It's only for a week."

"Three," Sarah corrected. "My parents have extended the time to make a reunion out of it. They've invited my whole entire family. Grandparents, uncles, aunts. Everybody. Three weeks. Can you believe it? Great way to end the summer. You're so lucky. Your parents aren't dragging you anywhere."

Lorrie's good mood was ruined. And then came the second punch.

"So I'm spending as much time with Joel as I can before I leave."

"Gee, thanks, Sarah." She sat up and hugged her knees.

Sarah was instantly contrite. She grabbed Lorrie's hand and pulled her back down beside her. "I want to spend time with you, too. Come with us tonight! It'll be fun. I'll introduce you to the guys in his band." She sounded excited.

"Maybe another time," Lorrie told her, careful to keep the anger and hurt out of her voice. She wasn't in the mood to fight. "Listen, I've gotta run."

"Before I leave, for sure, let's get together," Sarah called out as Lorrie crossed the field.

Lorrie lifted her arm in a backward wave. She didn't bother to turn around.

seventeen

If she kept shooting like this, she was going to be finished with the assignment by the middle of the week, Lorrie decided, glancing with satisfaction at the tall stack of completed prints.

Yesterday, after she left Sarah, she had worked until dark, taking pictures in downtown Bethesda of every texture she could find, and then she moved on to shapes.

The assignment to tell a story had been even easier. This morning, after her lesson with Thomas, Lorrie had been getting on her bike to go home when a Suburban rolled up, and before it was in the parking lot, she could hear girls squealing. When a whole gang of them bounded from the car and began jumping up and down around a little girl in braids and brand-new riding clothes, Lorrie had known that there was a story there.

The harried parents in charge of this birthday party had been pleased when Lorrie asked to take pictures and offered to send them a bunch of prints, so she had gotten to work. The eight-year-olds had flocked into the riding ring for a group lesson, and she had taken a couple of rolls of the kids working with Shane, their instructor.

In the darkroom, Lorrie sorted through the shots, smiling at the wide-eyed faces of the children, some of whom, it was clear, had never been so close to a horse before, much less a whole ringful of them.

Lorrie flipped through the stack. She'd been in here for hours, developing and then printing this birthday-party roll. Even before she laid them out on the counter, she was sure that the assignment was complete.

She thought then about printing some more, but when she looked at the clock, she was, as usual, startled by the passing of time. It was seven-thirty. She'd been down here all afternoon, except for a quick lunch break.

The house was quiet, but this time she wasn't worried. She'd seen Molly earlier, and, besides, she knew where to find her. Molly had been spending her evenings outside, on the bench in the little garden Lorrie was clearing. Often, Lorrie would join her and together they'd watch the sun set in the western sky.

This evening, when Lorrie came out, she found Molly asleep, her head to the side and her breath deep and gentle. She was wearing her ancient sweater, and her hands were folded loosely in her lap. She looked like she'd been sleeping for some time.

Lorrie decided not to wake her and went to work on the honeysuckle instead. It was oddly satisfying work to yank at the honeysuckle and toss it over her shoulder into what was getting to be a big tangled pile.

"You don't have to do that," Molly said behind her, sounding fully awake.

Lorrie tossed the vine into the pile and smiled at Molly. "I like it." She stepped back to examine her work. It was starting to look like a real garden again. Lorrie had freed a small patch of black-eyed Susans and a strangled row of daylilies that someone had planted against the fence. Farther down, she could see the white of daisies and the green of some low-growing cactuslike plant.

It was like a secret garden back here, just waiting for someone to dig it out. "Tell me some more about this Albert guy, Molly," she said, talking over her shoulder while she worked. She figured that, if she kept her tone real casual and made it sound like talking about Albert was the same as talking about the weather, maybe she'd find out something. Something good. Lorrie suspected there was a story here that Molly was keeping a secret. Why else would she have a picture of him in every room of the house?

Molly was quiet for a few moments before she answered. "What do you want to know?"

Crouching down to dig at the roots of the vine, Lorrie pivoted on her heels so that she could see Molly's face. "Everything," she said with a grin.

"He was a sweet man," Molly said, her voice soft and kind of dreamy. "A gentleman—a *gentle* man. You know, Lorrie, that's a good quality in a man, a certain gentleness."

Lorrie thought of Thomas. She shook the dirt from the roots. "Yes, Albert looks nice—in the pictures, I mean."

"He had a quiet passion about the things that he loved. Gardening. Children. Other people's children, that is. He and his wife never had any. I think that was a great disappointment to him."

"Hmm," Lorrie murmured.

Molly turned in her seat to survey the yard. "He loved coming here. You see, they lived in an apartment in the city, and this garden was his treasure. And the darkroom, of course." She chuckled, and Lorrie smiled at the deep, rumbling sound. "My, but he did love those silly flower pictures of his."

Lorrie rested for a moment on a big white rock she'd uncovered last week. "You didn't?"

Molly shrugged. "No, I can't say as I did. Still-lifes, flower arrangements, studio portraits"—she shook her head—"not enough drama for me. At least, that's what Albert said. 'You like action, don't you Molly?' he'd say. He once accused me of not appreciating beauty." She snorted.

Lorrie loved nature, but she, too, thought that pictures of flowers and sunsets were the dullest on earth.

They sat quietly for a few minutes. Lorrie observed the small patch she'd cleared and thought of all that was left to do. Of course, a lawn service could come in here and whip it into shape, but Lorrie didn't want that. She knew Molly

didn't, either.

"He worked like a fool back here, in that old gardening hat of his," Molly said, seeing Lorrie studying the yard.

"So he came alone?"

Molly's eyes flashed. "Yes, though he sometimes brought his wife, and the three of us would have dinner together on some of that fancy china you saw in there. But he had a key. He would come over when I was traveling."

Above them, a small woodpecker tapped at the bark of the old oak.

Molly looked thoughtful. "He found here a certain peace, something he didn't have anywhere else."

"Peace?"

"His wife was a strong-willed woman. She had a lot of interests. She came from a family with money. But she never understood Albert. She wanted more from him, wanted him to be someone he was not. That wore on him."

"So why didn't he leave her?"

Molly made a scoffing sound deep in the back of her throat. "You young people, you think it's that easy."

Lorrie immediately felt defensive. "I don't think it's so easy," she said sharply, "but I do think people have the right to be happy." She heard her mother's voice in her own.

"You do, do you?"

Lorrie didn't want to let it go. "I mean, if he wasn't happy, if he was really miserable, if he didn't love her . . ."

"I didn't say he didn't love her. I don't know a thing about that."

Lorrie went over and stomped down the honeysuckle pile. It popped right back up. What she needed was twine. Or a compost heap. Molly was right. Love was complicated, and marriage such a private thing. What could Molly, on the outside, possibly know about Albert and his wife? And yet . . . there was something that wasn't being said. "So, Molly, did you love him? Did you have an affair?"

Molly's eyes snapped in sudden anger. Lorrie was sure that if she'd been standing closer Molly would have reached over and swatted at her. "He was married," she spat. "For heaven's sake, Lorrie."

Recklessly, Lorrie continued. "That's what an affair is. One of you is married."

Molly glared at her. "We did *not* have an affair. Albert wasn't like that. I've just told you that he was a gentleman."

Lorrie met her gaze. "A gentle man. I know," she repeated kindly. She was truly interested in Albert. She didn't want to anger Molly.

"Well, he was." Molly shook her head in disgust. "Is that how it works these days? If you think you're unhappy and your life isn't turning out the way you think it should, then you get a divorce?"

Lorrie averted her face. Why had she brought up the topic anyway? Anything about divorce was bound to hit close to her heart. She'd always told herself that she was okay with her parents' splitting, but, to be honest, there was a part of her—a *big* part of her, maybe—that just wished they'd stuck it out and made it work. Like Albert had.

Maybe Molly sensed that Lorrie's mood had suddenly changed, because she patted the seat next to her so Lorrie would come and sit down. "In the beginning," she began, speaking softly, "our relationship was strictly professional. I annoyed him, I think, always asking questions and later, much later, telling him what I thought of some of his work. It was at a portrait studio in New York City, and I was his assistant. The shots were very staged. And dark. Heavy draperies in the background, thick rugs in front of the subjects. Dreadful stuff. We'll come across it, I'm sure. It's somewhere in this house of mine."

"I know the kind of pictures you mean. Sort of Victorian."

"Yes, exactly. But he seemed to like it. He always seemed older than I, but in reality we weren't that many years apart. He just got started earlier than I did. I had spent a year or two in secretarial school before I discovered photography."

"Would I have seen his work?"

Molly shook her head and shrugged. "I doubt it." Sounding wistful, she continued, "Your opening the dark-room has made me think about him again. He and his wife moved back to New York years ago, after Albert left the Library of Congress. His wife never liked it here. She had no interest in Albert's achievements as an archivist. She

always thought of Washington as a sleepy Southern town."
She sighed. "He is old now, like me, I guess."

Lorrie tried to picture Albert as a very old man, close in
age to Molly's eighty-some years.

Molly kept talking, caught up in the past. "He lacked
what you'd call gumption, that man. He was content with
documenting photos all day, but his passion was plants. He
longed to start a magazine on gardening. He could have
done it, too—his wife's family was quite comfortable and
money wasn't a problem—but he never did. That was his
big dream: to publish his own magazine with pages and
pages of beautiful flowers."

"But he didn't?"

"No. We talked about his plans for hours on end, but he
never gave it a try."

"That's sad."

"He asked me to marry him," she said quietly, her words
exploding into the air.

"*What?* You said—"

"No, early on. He asked me at lunch one day. We were
both in our twenties." She smiled, and Lorrie could imagine, for an instant, a much younger Molly. "I'd left the studio by then and was working for my first newspaper. My
assignments were small ones, but I was moving up. Shooting for the stars. I told him I'd give him my answer that
night after dinner. Looking back, as I've done many times
over the years, I wonder why I delayed it like that. Why
would the time between lunch and dinner make such a
difference?" Molly paused, and Lorrie waited for her to go
on. This was the best story she had told yet.

"Around four that afternoon, my editor called me into
his office. He had an overseas assignment and wanted to
know if I was interested. *Was I interested?* Do birds fly? Do

cows give milk?" She shook her head slowly, back and forth, remembering the day. "I can still *feel* it—how much I wanted that assignment." She looked at Lorrie. "I didn't even hesitate. I didn't think for a second of saying anything but yes. In fact, it wasn't until late that afternoon, when I was on my way home to pack, that I remembered Albert and his proposal."

"Uh-oh."

"Exactly." Molly's fingers played with the chipped buttons of her old sweater. "I was such a coward. Later that night, at dinner, I told him that I'd give him my decision when I returned. But when I came back, it was never for long. I went from assignment to assignment. I should have been ashamed of myself, but I wasn't."

"You were young," offered Lorrie.

"Yes, I was young. Then, one time, I returned to find that he'd met the woman he would marry."

"Wow." There didn't seem much more to say after that. The sun was setting, and Molly told Lorrie to watch the colors of the fence. "Look how the brown changes," she said. "You'll see it become a hundred different shades."

eighteen

The workday at Molly's underwent a drastic change once Elaine was finished with the law firm. Instead of quitting around noon, the three of them pushed on until five o'clock. It was a full day, and far too long for Molly. She was crankier than ever, but Elaine was convinced it was a schedule they'd all get used to.

Their days began in the upstairs storage room, where they were surrounded by boxes and heavy metal file cabinets filled with papers, prints, and negatives, all packed in special archival folders. Even when Lorrie opened the blinds to try to brighten up the room, it was still dreary. They all hated being there.

Molly quickly tired of the decision-making this kind of sorting involved. Sometimes they'd have been at it less than an hour when Molly, with a wave of her hand, would tell Elaine, "Just give it away. Give it to someone—I don't care who."

But it wasn't as easy as that. The papers and notebooks needed to be identified. Sometimes the boxes were clearly marked, but other times Molly had to pore over her own difficult script, some of it fifty years old, and try to place when and where she had written it. It was hard, tiring work, and Molly didn't like it.

Lorrie knew her stepmother was frustrated with how slowly things were going. One evening, she overheard Elaine saying to her dad, "Molly said she wanted to do this, but now she seems to be backing off completely. She's not cooperating at all."

This was after Elaine had brought up once again the subject of Molly's new home. Elaine was excited because she'd received a call from the resident manager that an apartment was now available.

"We have to go see it, Molly," Elaine insisted that morning, as soon as they joined her in the kitchen, where she was nursing a cup of tea.

But Molly had her mind made up. "I can't live on the third floor. Elevators are always breaking down."

Elaine was clearly exasperated. "Molly, what are you talking about? You specifically requested *not* to be put on the ground floor. You said you were afraid of break-ins. We were sitting right here at this kitchen table when we went over all of this."

Lorrie saw Molly lift her chin and get that stubborn look in her eye.

"I believe I've changed my mind," Molly said stiffly.

Elaine tossed her pen down on the table and stood up. "For goodness' sakes, Molly," she said, sounding angry. "You can't stay here forever."

"The heck I can't."

The two of them glared at each other for a long minute. Finally, Elaine turned on her heel. "I think I'd better take a walk around the block before I say anything I'll regret."

"Suit yourself," Molly retorted.

Lorrie shifted uncomfortably in her seat. She felt caught in the middle, and she didn't like it one bit. The front door shut with a firm bang, and she and Molly were alone. Molly busied herself cleaning the teapot and cups until Elaine came back in. The apartment wasn't mentioned again.

....

For the next few days, Molly resisted the work and Elaine grew more frustrated, but by the week's end, a new pattern was establishing itself. Lorrie and Elaine worked with Molly for an hour or so in the morning, and then, just as she was getting fed up, they'd leave her with a small task while they went downstairs to continue preparing the walls for painting. Left on her own with a notebook to browse through or a small box of prints, Molly was productive. Later in the day, she would hand Elaine a brief description of the materials.

Despite this uneasy peace, the week ended on an angry note over another touchy topic: housepainting. Elaine was sure that Molly had originally agreed to hire a small crew of professional painters, if she was still here in September, but now she was balking at the idea.

"I don't want strangers in my house," she insisted.

"But, Molly, Lorrie and I can't paint every room. There's just no way. Lorrie has school, and I have commitments—new clients who want to meet with me."

But Molly wouldn't discuss it. This time it was she who left the room to go cool off, and Elaine and Lorrie were by themselves in the kitchen.

"I just can't bend on this one," Elaine said.

Lorrie knew that quitting her job had been hard for Elaine, and that Molly's sudden opposition to everything wasn't making it any easier. "Maybe she'll change her mind," she offered lamely.

Elaine wiped down the countertops and table. Everything was dusty from the work they'd been doing. "You and I both know that Molly Price is one of the most stubborn people on the face of the earth."

"Okay, so she's a tiny bit stubborn," said Lorrie, trying to get Elaine to smile, "but even stubborn people change their minds sometimes."

Elaine reached for the broom. "Let's hope you're right, because I am not climbing up on any scaffolding to paint that staircase wall. And," she added quickly, "neither are you."

When Molly still hadn't come out of her study by the end of the afternoon, Lorrie decided to stick around, promising Elaine she'd be home before total darkness.

She had an idea. Earlier in the week, she'd discovered a lawn mower in the shed. Molly had told her that it worked, that the kid who cut the front yard used it every once in a while. Now Lorrie pulled it out of the rusty old shed and examined it. She wanted to mow the backyard, and this would be perfect. The grass was way too tall for a fancy mower like the one her dad and Elaine had. That had its own mulcher, and when the grass got too high, it kept jamming up. This sturdy machine looked like it could cut through anything.

But first she had to go through the entire yard and pick up the branches that had been falling for years. Then she spent another half-hour trimming along the rock borders so she wouldn't run over them. Finally, she was ready to cut the grass.

The engine started right up, and she began mowing, stopping every fifteen minutes or so to empty the grass bag. She was dumping it for the last time when she saw Molly standing on the back porch. There was a big, wide smile on her face.

Together they admired the transformed yard. The low grass gave it an entirely new look.

"I feel like I've stepped back in time," Molly said happily. "I almost expect to see Albert coming around the corner wearing that floppy hat of his."

In a funny way, Lorrie did, too.

Arm in arm, they walked around the yard, passing their bench and looping around the oak tree, once, then again. Molly pointed out the beds still buried in weeds. For someone who didn't like flowers, she knew an awful lot of flower names.

"It smells good," Molly sighed, breathing in the scent of cut grass and the remaining honeysuckle.

"It sure does."

Lorrie had never seen Molly look quite as happy as she did that evening. Lorrie knew then, as they walked across the expanse of lawn to return to the house, that Molly would never leave this place. Not this fall. Not ever.

....

After their late dinner at the deli, things between Lorrie and Thomas changed. There was an ease now, a new friendliness between them.

On Sunday, out riding, Lorrie told Thomas about the garden. "You're the only other person who knows," she said.

"Not even Elaine?"

"Well, she'll know on Monday, when she sees I've mowed it. I guess now it won't be such a secret place."

"You don't have to invite her out there."

Lorrie laughed. "No, and, besides, she might not even notice. Suddenly she's obsessed, like getting Molly moved out is the most important thing in her life."

"I guess right now it is."

"My dad says to give her some time. He says quitting her job was a bigger deal than she anticipated."

They talked back and forth as their horses walked down the path, Bullet ahead of Niki.

Thomas turned in his saddle. "I saw you taking pictures last week of the birthday party. You looked like a real pro."

Lorrie grinned. She hadn't even known Thomas was watching her that day. "That was fun. But the last assignment's hard, the one on emotion. How do you take pictures of emotion?"

"Maybe you could get a picture of Elaine and Molly arguing."

"Yeah, that's an idea."

A couple of riders came toward them on the trail. Lorrie pulled Niki over to the side to let them pass. Thomas backed up and reached down to pat Niki's neck.

Shifting in their places, their horses stayed side by side. "I'm really stumped on this assignment, Thomas. Give me some ideas. I've gone out twice to shoot it and I've come back with nothing."

"You can always go for people crying, if that's not too easy an out," Thomas suggested.

"I'm desperate. Where are people crying?"

Thomas kicked his horse forward. "Why not go downtown to the Vietnam Veterans Memorial?"

Lorrie thought about that for a moment as they walked along. She ducked under a low branch. Her history teacher last year had talked about it, the long wall filled with the names of those who had died or were missing in action. It'd been designed by some student, a woman who'd won a contest or something. "Yeah, that might work," Lorrie agreed. She looked up through the trees. "And the light's good today." It was slightly overcast, not too sunny. She told Thomas about Ms. Hanson, her history teacher, as they rode along.

After a while, Thomas pulled his horse to a stop, and Lorrie did the same. They were standing close, so close that Lorrie could have reached over and touched Thomas's leg. The woods, thick and cool, surrounded them.

"I'd love to take the day off and go downtown with you," Thomas said.

Lorrie felt her lips widen into a silly smile. She looked down and pretended to pull a twig out of Niki's mane. "That would be fun."

"But I've got appointments all day, and Frances called in sick."

"And there's no one else to bring in?" she asked, looking at him directly now.

Thomas shook his head. "Not today. People are starting to go on vacation. I'm outta here next week myself."

Lorrie's smile faded.

Thomas slid off his horse and steadied hers while she dismounted. "Let's walk a little," he said, taking her hand in his and both sets of reins in the other.

They strolled along the path, their horses following behind. Thomas talked about his parents' vacation house up in Maine, and how they ate lobster on the beach, and how cold the water was. He promised to bring her back one of the starfishes that could be found clinging to the rocks under the dock in low tide. Lorrie loved hearing him talk. She wished she had the whole day to spend like this, holding hands and walking in the woods.

Their privacy ended when trees gave way to soccer fields. Cars passed, and kids were screaming in the playground.

Before they got back on their horses, Thomas turned to her. "About your next lesson. Shane is supposed to take some of my appointments—"

Lorrie was already shaking her head. "No, no thanks. I'll just wait for you to come back."

"I'm special?" Thomas asked with a grin.

"Yeah, you're special," Lorrie said shyly.

"Good." Taking a step closer, he reached out and pulled a leaf from her hair. They both watched it float to the ground. It was yellow.

"An early sign that fall is coming," Thomas said. He threaded his fingers through hers.

She'd spent a lot of time this summer thinking about Thomas, and one of the things she'd thought about most was kissing him. She caught herself sometimes, when they were standing close like this, looking at his mouth and wanting so badly to touch it. She longed to feel his lips against her cheek, under her fingertips, on her own mouth.

Now she knew it was about to happen. She wanted to moisten her lips. She wanted a drink of water. She wanted to run across the field and kick the ball with the middle-school boys who were playing there.

She did none of those things. She stood still and heard the cars driving by, the horses' hooves shuffling behind her, and the running water in the creek. She heard all those things until Thomas's lips touched hers, and then she didn't hear a thing.

Much too quickly, his lips were gone, and quicker still, he was back on his horse. Her cheeks, she knew, were flushed, and her hands felt empty. She wished she could have the whole last hour back again.

nineteen

On the subway ride to the memorial, Lorrie couldn't stop thinking about Thomas. She couldn't stop smiling, either, and strangers on the train kept smiling back at her.

She had no idea where this whole thing with Thomas was going. She knew her dad would have a problem with her dating a guy in college, but for now, she didn't care. He'd promised to bring her a starfish, as corny as that sounded.

She'd wanted to talk to Sarah, but Sarah wasn't at the stables yet, and Lorrie, still kind of angry at her, was hesitant to drop by her home. So she'd e-mailed a note instead, telling her about the kiss. It seemed silly to e-mail someone who lived half a mile away, but it wasn't a bad way to get in touch with someone you weren't sure you wanted to talk to face-to-face. Lorrie didn't even know how often Sarah checked her e-mail these days. Last year, they'd written back and forth all the time.

The streets were packed with tourists who'd come to see the nation's capital. Lorrie weaved her way through them to get to the memorial, down at the end of the Mall. The Wall, as it was called, was built into a small knoll and tucked out of view, so Lorrie saw the line of people out front long before she saw the memorial itself. She took her place in the line of somber visitors who spoke in hushed voices as they inched closer to the shiny black granite Wall.

When the memorial was in sight, Lorrie realized that Ms. Hanson had been right. There was something arresting about this place. It was all the names, thousands of them carved deep into the tall panels of the Wall.

The line crept forward, breaking up as people stopped to finger a name or set down a letter or a small stuffed toy. People were quieter now, the whispering replaced by silence or gentle crying. A few feet ahead of Lorrie, a woman held a piece of paper against a name and rubbed it with a pencil. Her cheeks were wet with tears.

Lorrie reached for her camera. Okay, this was it. This was the kind of emotion that would work perfectly for the fourth assignment. All she had to do was focus and snap. It would be easy. She could be finished in minutes.

She lifted the camera to her eye. The woman was now sobbing, her shoulders heaving up and down. A man, also crying, stepped over and cradled her in his arm. Lorrie wondered who they were crying for. A son? A nephew? The woman's brother? A neighborhood boy?

Lorrie lowered the camera. The shot was there, but she couldn't take it.

She walked on, and stopped feet away from an even more poignant picture. Three men, obviously all veterans in their jackets and hats, stood close together in sober silence. One of them held a small American flag, which he gently placed at the base of the Wall.

Lorrie kept walking. The special feeling she'd had after Thomas kissed her was completely gone. Why had she come here *today*?

Molly had said to shoot emotion, a single dominant emotion, but she'd never said it had to be sadness. Lorrie remembered that there was a merry-go-round over by the Smithsonian. She was some distance from the sounds of crying and sadness when she realized that she didn't need to walk all the way to the other end of the Mall: There were kids right here. Half a dozen of them played tag while their parents gathered on a nearby bench, the shiny black wall of the memorial behind them.

Lorrie used her zoom to tighten the shot so that it held only the playing children. She snapped one of a girl laughing, her dark hair falling on her brown shoulders. Her sister jumped high for a swooping pigeon, and Lorrie increased the shutter speed to capture the girl in the air.

From her new location, Lorrie tried the Wall again. It was easier now. She was too far away to hear the sobs or read the handwritten notes left behind. She took pictures of a middle-aged man with his head bowed, and some of a long-haired boy around her own age stretching up to rub a name. Then she focused on a small boy placing a brown teddy bear with a white card tied to its neck at the Wall's base. Keeping the camera to her eye, she stepped forward until the words on the card came into focus. "Grandpa," it said, in the messy script of a young child.

Staying at what was still a safe distance, Lorrie easily shot three rolls. She packed her camera into her bag and was about to leave when she remembered that her history teacher had an older brother who was killed in Vietnam. Lorrie had held in her hands the last letter he'd mailed home: "It's very hot here but I am fine. Keep writing."

His name was Jerry. Gerald Alton the Third. He'd signed his letter that way, too. Lorrie remembered it because it had been funny, and she had wondered if it had been a joke.

She got back in line, stopping this time to look up Gerald Alton in the directory that identified the panel the name was on. She took a picture of his name in the book. Then, like the people around her, she did a rubbing.

Feeling the letters under her fingertips, she thought of Molly's soldier. Where on the Wall was he?

· ·

When she got home, she found a note from her dad that said dinner was in the fridge and he and Elaine would be home around eight. Lorrie took a quick shower and then, eager to get into the darkroom with today's work, scribbled her own note and rode over to Molly's.

It was five o'clock, a time of day Molly enjoyed spending in her backyard, so that's where Lorrie went to look for her when she couldn't find her in the house.

"Molly?" she called as she stepped outside.

There were signs that she'd been there. A teacup had been left on the bench, and Lorrie was sure Molly had trimmed some weeds from around the tree trunk, where a pair of clippers still lay. Lorrie started to feel panicked. Irrationally, she called out Molly's name a few more times, even looking into the dark and crowded shed, but the elderly woman was not around.

Back in the house, Lorrie raced from room to room, shouting for Molly and then freezing every moment or so to listen for a response. But the house was still and quiet and, seemingly, empty. Completely unnerved, Lorrie paced from the kitchen to the front door and back. In the foyer, in the living room, on the dining-room table, she searched for a note—anything that might indicate where Molly had gone.

She wanted to call Elaine, but her parents were out and Lorrie hadn't memorized Elaine's pager or cell-phone numbers. As she searched the house one more time before going home for the numbers, Lorrie tried to calm herself. Molly must have had friends that Lorrie didn't know about. Perhaps one of them had come by to take her out to dinner.

This scenario seemed less likely when Lorrie found Molly's handbag up in her office and her Keds by her bed.

The only place she hadn't searched thoroughly was the basement, but the lights were out, and when she'd run down earlier, she'd concluded that Molly would never have been able to find her way in the dark. This time, however, Lorrie noticed something she hadn't seen before. Though the lights in the darkroom were off, the door was just slightly open. This was odd: Lorrie always shut the door tightly, so that the odor of chemicals wouldn't seep up into the rest of the house.

"Molly?" Lorrie stepped tentatively into the darkened room. She turned on the light. Molly was there. She'd been sitting in total darkness, perched on a stool.

Lorrie gasped, "Molly! Molly, what are you doing?"

She looked up at Lorrie and blinked. "Hello there, young lady." Her voice sounded strange—and she looked strange, too. Her hair was down on her shoulders, making her look wild. She was still in her nightgown, and she wore her green sweater over it—but backward. Lorrie felt a peculiar relief that she had her slippers on.

"Molly. What are you doing down here?"

Molly looked about her. "I come here often," she said simply.

Frightened, Lorrie put her arm around her friend. "Come on, let's go upstairs."

Molly ignored her. "I believe we have work to do, do we not?"

She doesn't even sound like herself. "Work?"

"Yes. Aren't those prints due by Tuesday? You can't call yourself a professional if you don't respect deadlines."

"What are you talking about, Molly? My assignments aren't due Tuesday. And I'm not a professional anything. I'm only fifteen. I'm in high school." She fought a rising panic that was making her start to choke on her words. "Molly, please. Let's go upstairs."

"No, thank you. I think I'll just stay here and watch."

"Watch what?" Lorrie was scared. She glanced at the phone on the wall and wished that her dad and Elaine were around. They'd know what to do.

"Don't let me stop you, precious." Molly never called her that. And she had the oddest expression on her face, too. She was looking at Lorrie as if this all made perfect sense.

Lorrie tried another tactic. "Something's different today, Molly," she began, trying to appear nonchalant as she pulled prints out of the drawer and tossed them on the counter. "Why are you calling me 'young lady' and 'precious' instead of my real name?"

Molly was silent.

"You *do* know my name, don't you?"

Molly squinted and gave her a long look. For a moment, the fuzziness was gone. "Of course I know your name," she snapped. "You're Lorrie, Lora Taylor. L-o-r-a."

Lorrie felt her shoulders fall in relief. "Okay. You had me scared there for a minute." Dropping to her knees at Molly's feet, she implored, "What were you doing down here in the dark?"

"Darkrooms are supposed to be dark. Now let's get started," Molly said, pointing to the countertop where Lorrie had left the prints.

Lorrie tried again. "Wouldn't you rather go outside and sit in the garden? It's a beautiful evening."

Molly shook her head. "I've been weeding all day, and I'm tired now. I think I'll rest while you work."

"Okay," Lorrie reluctantly agreed, "but only after I get you into a comfortable chair." She left the room and returned quickly with a padded armchair from the dining room. "Let me help you." Molly felt so feeble beneath her hands, it was surprising she'd managed to get down the stairs.

Molly sank into the chair and had her eyes closed before Lorrie had unpacked her bag. She pulled out the rolls from the Vietnam Memorial. It was almost better that Molly was here, where Lorrie could keep a close eye on her. She looked so peaceful.

Lorrie watched Molly carefully while she developed her film. The old photographer slept on, her breathing so regular and relaxed that Lorrie worked for almost two hours. Finally, she thought it best to get Molly out of that chair.

"Molly, I'm done in here." She gave her shoulder a gentle shake. Molly didn't awaken.

Lorrie shook a little bit harder, but Molly was in a deep sleep, much deeper than Lorrie had realized. When she finally opened her eyes, the enormity of the problem was clear.

"Albert? Has he left the lights on again? I'm always coming down here to turn them off."

"Albert." The name stuck in Lorrie's throat. "Molly, are you dreaming? Wake up." She shook her shoulder again, but there was no need. Molly's eyes were wide open.

"His wife called. She's expecting him for dinner. 'No lateness this time, Albert,'" Molly mimicked in a high nasal voice. "She was in a real snit, but who can blame her? He's always tardy, that man. I told her, 'Well, you're married to a man who's always late. You should know that by now.'"

Lorrie reached for the phone. She was really frightened. Something was terribly wrong—had been wrong, too, for the whole time she'd been here. Why hadn't she done something *hours* ago?

She began turning the old-fashioned rotary dial. Molly was looking wildly around her, talking total gibberish now.

"Elaine, this is Lorrie," Lorrie said into the answering machine that picked up at home. "I'm over at Molly's. Something's wrong. I'm going to call 911. Please come—" Molly was pushing herself up and out of the chair. Lorrie tossed down the phone and threw herself across the room, managing to catch Molly in her arms as she collapsed.

....

The ambulance seemed to take forever. EMTs came through the open back door and found her in the basement, holding Molly's head in her lap. Suddenly she was pushed to the side and out of the room. She heard them talking and talking, ripping open packages and connecting tubes.

Some woman with a clipboard asked her a bunch of questions that she didn't know the answers to. Then Elaine was there. Lorrie heard her telling the woman with the clipboard about medications and health insurance and Molly's hospital visit just a couple of weeks ago. Lorrie sneaked away and climbed onto the washing machine in the darkened laundry room. She stayed there as the stretcher went up the stairs. She didn't move even when the house was quiet.

Her dad came for her, and the first thing he did was take her in his arms and hold her while she cried. Afterward, on the ride home, he talked a lot, but she only heard one word.

Coma. It was the same word that everyone had used before her grandmother died. Lorrie had been very young. "She's still in a coma," she remembered hearing her mother say when people called. And then, a long time later, when her grandmother died, her mother and everyone else said, "She never came out of it."

Lorrie couldn't bear the thought of this happening to Molly.

Around five in the morning, she heard the front door open. It was Elaine. Lorrie's dad came out of his room at the same time, and the three of them gathered in the kitchen.

"Apparently she's had a stroke," Elaine said, her voice almost a whisper. "They'll run tests. Right now, there's no reason to be anything but optimistic."

The words meant nothing to Lorrie.

Elaine took her hand and squeezed it. "All her vital signs are good. It's as if she is asleep. She's so lucky you were there."

Lorrie turned to go back to bed. She'd heard enough.

"Lorrie," Elaine went on, "go see her. You'll feel better if you do."

Lorrie kept her back turned. She had cried earlier. She felt numb now.

"Lora?" This time it was her dad.

She left the room and climbed the steps, ignoring their calls to her. Didn't they understand anything? This shouldn't have happened. She'd been there for two hours before she called the ambulance. If she'd done something immediately, maybe Molly would be all right.

twenty

Lorrie's first impression when she walked into Molly's house was that it was entirely too bright. Elaine had been here all day yesterday and the day before, dismantling the living room and the downstairs study. With Molly out of the house, they could strip the entire first floor for painting. The blinds and curtains were off all the windows, the furniture was pushed to the center of the rooms, and the living-room walls were bare of the pictures, which they'd left hanging to make the house feel more comfortable for Molly.

Elaine greeted her at the door. "It looks bad, I know, but if we work fast, we can get all this done before Molly comes home."

Lorrie didn't say anything. Molly was still in a coma, and the doctors weren't saying a thing about her coming home.

"Can you help me with the drop cloths?" Elaine asked, leading Lorrie into the living room.

The living-room walls were in worse shape than Lorrie had realized. Her job for the day was to tape and spackle the holes and cracks.

"Her pictures are upstairs," Elaine said, tucking the plastic sheet under a leg of the sofa. "We'll get everything back the way it was, don't worry."

Lorrie still said nothing. She couldn't seem to get the dialogue that was going on nonstop in her head to travel down to her tongue.

Elaine, on the other hand, couldn't seem to stop talking. "If we can put in some long days, I think we can start painting next week."

Lorrie plugged in the radio and got started. Working made her feel better. She took few breaks. Hour after hour, she sanded and scraped and spackled.

When Elaine quit at five to go visit Molly in the hospital, Lorrie stayed. The house was quiet. A couple of times she was sure she heard Molly shuffling into the room. But when she turned around, the doorway was empty, and she had to remember all over again that Molly lay still in a hospital bed a mile from here.

Lorrie had more work to do on the walls, but she was tired of climbing up and down the stepladder. She was eager to start on the living-room mantelpiece. This was a whole project in itself. She set a fan into the open window and brushed paint remover onto a small area of the mantel's elaborate woodwork. The strong chemical lifted up layers and layers of old paint.

Molly will like this, Lorrie found herself thinking as she scraped paint off a carved cluster of grapes. For the first time since Molly was carried out on the stretcher, Lorrie was thinking in terms of her return.

When Elaine came by around nine to tear Lorrie away from her work, Lorrie told her about hearing Molly's slippered footfalls.

"That happened to me, too," Elaine admitted, pulling

the front door shut behind them. "But today it was better. I keep thinking of how pleased she'll be when she gets back and how, if we work hard, we can give her a wonderful homecoming."

"Homecoming." Lorrie liked how that sounded.

....

The work went quickly. Elaine and Lorrie started early. They stopped late. They turned up the radio and pounded and sanded and made a big, big mess. The harder they worked, the better they both felt about the whole situation.

Together they finished all the prep work on the first floor, except for the high ceilings of the hallway. Elaine was planning to bring in a professional to help out. He would begin with the exterior, putting fresh white paint on the brick and black on the shutters.

"Will it be okay with Molly?" Lorrie asked late Friday afternoon, remembering that argument. Elaine was sitting on the work stool in the middle of the living room. Lorrie had grown used to the idea of the two of them tearing the house apart to paint, but something didn't feel right about bringing in outside people when Molly wasn't home.

"There's one guy, a man Molly has hired before—she mentioned him last week. I'm not going to bring in a whole staff of people, if that's what you're worried about."

Lorrie ran her hand over the grapevine design on the front of the mantelpiece. "It's just that you know how Molly is—"

"Yes, I know how Molly is. She's the one who gave me his number."

Lorrie relaxed. She glanced around her, imagining the room as it would look when it was done. "Molly will be pleased."

Elaine stood up, brushed off her dusty clothes, and shook her hair out of the short ponytail she wore when she worked. "Do you want to come to the hospital with me?" Her tone was casual, as it was each evening around this time when she asked Lorrie this same question.

Lorrie shook her head. There was no need to say more. The only way she could deal with this whole thing was to work on Molly's house.

She couldn't talk about it to anyone. She'd e-mailed another message to Sarah, but Sarah apparently wasn't checking her mail. "I'm going to hang around here a little longer. Maybe start sanding the molding that runs up the steps."

"I'll come by and get you on my way home, and then your dad and I are going to go out to a movie. You can come if you want," she added. "Maybe you and Sarah—"

"Sarah's leaving tomorrow, and I'm sure she plans to spend the evening with Joel."

After Elaine left, Lorrie went up to Molly's office. She came up here in the evening sometimes, once she was alone.

The blinds were raised and the room was bright, so Lorrie didn't bother to flip on the light. She just wanted to sit here for a while and look at Molly's pictures on the walls. This room was still untouched.

She swiveled in Molly's chair the way that Molly used to. She picked up Molly's pen and held it between her fingers. She shut her eyes and breathed in the faint scent of talc that was Molly. The next thing she knew, Elaine was down in the foyer, calling her name.

She heard Elaine go through the house. "Lorrie, are you in the darkroom?" she called at the top of the basement stairs.

But Lorrie hadn't been down there all week, not since

they'd picked Molly up off the cold concrete floor. She didn't think she could bear to return there, not until Molly was back home.

· · · · · · · · · · · · · · · · · · · ·

Later that night, Lorrie reached for the phone by her bed and called her mom. She'd called her three or four times already, just to hear her voice, to hear her talk about things that had nothing to do with Molly.

But this time it was Lorrie who couldn't stop talking. She told her mother about everything that had happened since she'd moved back here. Some of it she'd said before, but she repeated it all. She couldn't seem to stop herself. She told her mom about how Sarah was never around. She told her about Thomas and the lessons and that he'd kissed her last Sunday morning. She told her all about Molly, and about Elaine's offer for Lorrie to do the interviews, and about the garden out back. And, finally, she told her about Molly's stroke, and how she'd been there and had waited all that time before she'd done anything.

"Oh, Lorrie," her mother said, so gently that just her tone made Lorrie feel like crying. "I would have done the same thing. Anyone would have." She said some more stuff that Lorrie didn't really hear. "Listen, darling, you're being too hard on yourself."

After that call, Lorrie started to feel a little better. Maybe it was pathetic to be fifteen and still need to talk to your mom, but she didn't care.

She turned out the light when she heard her dad on the steps, so that he'd think she was asleep. Suddenly she was dead tired. A week spent worrying about Molly and doing the hard work of preparing to paint a house caught up with her. When her dad popped his head in the door, she didn't have to pretend to be too sleepy to respond.

············

By the beginning of the next week, Lorrie and Elaine were putting primer on the walls, and Lorrie felt every muscle in her body complaining. She had never been so sore in her life.

It wasn't like she'd never painted a room before, either. But this was different. At Molly's, she and Elaine put in eight or ten hours a day, and with the high ceilings and the elaborate molding along the perimeters of the rooms, Lorrie was constantly climbing up and down ladders and reaching over and back and up and down. Every part of her body was getting a workout.

Elaine told her to take more breaks, that Molly wasn't in any hurry over at the hospital, where she was still sleeping peacefully, but that comment just made Lorrie want to push harder.

A pain shot through her right wrist. She'd been holding the paint roller all day. She ignored it and refilled her paint tray. "I'm just going to finish this wall before lunch," she told Elaine, who had given up trying to reason with her.

············

Late Thursday, her dad surprised her and Elaine by making a big announcement at dinner. "I've been offered reservations at the Greenbrier for this weekend."

Elaine was thrilled. "Oh, that sounds wonderful! A weekend off from everything!" she exclaimed. "We can go early tomorrow. We can take off around three. Okay, Lorrie?"

Lorrie put down her fork and thought about how to say

what was on her mind. She had to choose her words carefully. The last thing she wanted to do was go away for the weekend to some ritzy resort with her dad and Elaine. The day trip had been fine, but not this. Not an entire weekend. And not now.

But getting out of it was going to be tricky. With Sarah gone, she had no place else to stay, and her mom was all the way on the West Coast, too far for Lorrie to visit. What she wanted to do was to stay home alone. That was not an idea her dad would easily agree to, but Lorrie stood firm. Her best argument was that she used to baby-sit weekends for a family back in Pennsylvania, so it wasn't like she was afraid to be alone at night. Her other argument was that she would be sixteen in November—and sixteen wasn't twelve or thirteen. Sixteen was old enough to spend the night by herself.

She had been on the debate team at her old high school. She knew how to argue calmly and logically. Plus, she wanted to stay home just as much as her dad and Elaine wanted to go off to this place in the mountains where they could hike and sleep and play golf.

Finally, later that night, her dad came into her room. "We have agreed to leave you here," he said. "I've called your mother and discussed it with her. And then I called Marsha Brooks and Carol Stein," he said, naming two women who'd been family friends for as long as Lorrie could remember. "Both Marsha and Carol are going to call you each evening and again in the morning. If you have any problems, either of them can be here in three minutes. And you are not to go in the pool without telling them first and calling them when you get out."

Lorrie counted to five. That was a trick she had learned in debating, and right now it kept her from whining about how stupid this sounded. By the time she got to five, she'd decided that this was the best deal she was going to get. If she argued even a little, she would blow it. "I don't like that pool rule, but I agree," she said calmly. She tried not to sound too excited.

"I still think it would be better if you came with us," her father couldn't help adding. He had a worried look on his face.

"Oh, Dad, where's your sense of romance? Stop acting like you're too old to have fun," Lorrie teased.

His face broke into a smile. "This is a little spur-of-the-moment for me. It didn't even occur to me that you wouldn't want to come."

Lorrie kissed her dad on the cheek and walked him to the door. "Dad, I'm a teenager. I'm not supposed to want to spend the weekend with my parents. And, besides, this is good for you—doing something for once that you haven't spent weeks planning. Do something wild and reckless. Maybe you can try bungee jumping while you're there."

He looked horrified at the thought. "Elaine will have her pager and her cell on twenty-four hours a day. You can call us anytime."

Lorrie groaned loudly, but she waited for him to turn his back before she rolled her eyes. Then she forgot all about her parents and thought about herself. Two whole days without anybody to bother her. And they were leaving money for food and shopping. She did a happy dance on her carpeted floor.

twenty-one

The first thing Lorrie did on Saturday morning was something she could do only when no one else was around. Earlier that spring, when the pool was going in, Sarah had sent her a bikini that she'd bought and never had the nerve to wear in public. It was a gag gift, and Lorrie had stuck it in the back of her drawer.

But today, with the pool and the house all to herself, Lorrie figured, *Why not? Who's here to see?* She slipped it on, checked in the mirror to make sure it was decent enough to wear in her backyard, and grabbed a fresh towel.

It wasn't yet ten, but the flagstone was hot beneath her bare feet as she padded around, in and out of the house several times, before she was set up for a day. Finally, she pulled the chaise into the sun, covered it with a towel, and stretched out.

The bikini seemed even smaller outside, with the sun hitting places it'd never shone on before, but it felt good. The long hours working at Molly's and the swimming she'd been doing had left her fit. Now to get some color.

She shut her eyes and pulled the straps down off her shoulders a little. She listened to the breeze in the trees, the shouts of kids playing two doors up, the buzz of a distant lawn mower. She drifted in and out of sleep, waking up fully only once, to reapply sunblock.

This was how she'd envisioned the summer when she'd told her mother back in May that she wanted to move in with her dad right away rather than wait until just before school started. She'd thought it would be exactly like this—lazing around the pool, having the house to herself, doing nothing, talking to no one but Sarah, sleeping and eating in her bathing suit.

She lay there for hours, turning around a couple of times to tan evenly, finishing the last hundred pages of her book before pulling the chair into the shade. Her thoughts drifted, stopping now and then at the oddest places, like last year at school, with Bart, and this summer, with Thomas in the woods. She thought of her mom, and then her dad and Elaine, and how she was getting used to this whole thing. She wondered what Sarah did when she was out with Joel. Then, finally, she remembered Molly.

Molly! Her eyes flew open, and she sat up. Today would be the first day since she went into the hospital that no one came to visit her. Lorrie tried to shrug off the thought, getting up slowly and running the hose over her shoulders. The water felt freezing cold, then it felt good.

She didn't want to think about Molly, she admitted, turning off the hose. This was *her* day, a day to focus on herself.

But Molly kept popping into her head. Molly snapping at her the day they met. Molly in the garden wearing her old green sweater in the July heat. Molly showing her the darkroom for the first time.

Even though Lorrie hadn't been to the hospital, she could picture the scene in her mind's eye. Molly lying in bed, alone, covered in one of those thick white hospital sheets, the shiny metal bars of the bed drawn up around her, some machine making noises off to the side. Lorrie wondered if she had one of those pitchers of ice water that all patients get and whether she had flowers on her windowsill, filling the room with their sweet scent.

Lorrie sat on the edge of the pool, her feet in the water. It was getting late, close to five now. The day had gone by quickly. She went inside to shower and change.

Elaine hadn't talked much about Molly, except to say she was in a peaceful sleep that the doctors were hopeful she would wake from. Elaine spoke with her, whispered to her, Lorrie knew, with the belief that Molly heard.

Lorrie didn't know if it was true, but what if Molly *could* hear? What if she knew that a whole day was passing without anyone coming to see her? It seemed so cruel.

Lorrie had to go.

. . . .

Straddling the bike between her legs, Lorrie stared at the brick building for a long time. It was big and ugly, and Lorrie had hated it since she was a little girl and had gone there to have her tonsils out. The hospital had changed since then. It had a helicopter pad right out front for trauma patients. Lorrie hoped that Molly couldn't see this from her room. What was she thinking? Molly hadn't opened her eyes since she'd been in there.

Lorrie lingered on the sidewalk, watching the light play off the red brick. She looked at her watch. Shadows were lengthening as evening approached. It was Molly and Lorrie's favorite time of day.

Lorrie rode to the visitors' entrance. Before she could change her mind, she locked her bike and stepped up to the automatic door.

Room 401 was easy to find. Too easy. Lorrie entered and came upon an empty bed. For a heart-stopping moment, she thought it was Molly's, but then she saw a second bed, behind the curtain.

Lorrie was glad she was alone. She couldn't help crying at the sight of Molly, her face so pale, her small body so fragile beneath the white sheet. After a few minutes, Lorrie tiptoed closer. What Elaine had said was true—Molly just looked like she was asleep. Lorrie listened to the soft sounds of her breathing and watched her chest rise gently up and down.

The noise was soothing, and Lorrie found herself pacing her own breaths to Molly's. There was plenty of room at the foot of the bed. She sat down.

Staring at her friend's face, she asked herself, *Why was I so scared to come here? It's just Molly sleeping, like she's done so many times before, out in the garden or on the side porch.*

She wondered if she should try to talk to her, to tell her she was there. She cleared her throat and tried to speak, but she felt silly. Instead, she reached for Molly's hand and decided that this time, this first time, she'd talk to Molly from inside her head.

Hey, Molly, she said, raising her voice in her head, if you could do that. *I'm so happy to see you. I wish you were home. Elaine and I have some surprises for you that I bet you'll like.*

She squeezed the frail hand in hers. *We're about to start painting with those colors you picked out.*

Lorrie stopped "talking." She remembered the last day, down in the darkroom.

I'm sorry, I'm so sorry that I didn't do anything sooner.

She stroked Molly's palm. It was warm and soft. Lorrie hadn't uttered a single word since she'd come into the room, but by the time a nurse entered a couple of minutes later, she felt like she and Molly had had a real visit.

"Is this your grandmother?" the middle-aged woman asked.

"No." Lorrie's voice sounded squeaky. It wasn't just that she hadn't spoken in here. She hadn't said a word out loud since her parents had called this morning. "She's a friend. My stepmother's been coming in all the other days."

"I'm only here weekends," the woman said. She picked up Molly's wrist and took her pulse. "All her vital signs are good. It's good for her to have someone here with her, talking to her, holding her hand."

Lorrie stood up as the nurse left the room. She'd promised her dad that she'd be home well before dark. Leaning toward Molly, she whispered, out loud this time, "I'll stay longer next time." She gave Molly a quick kiss on the forehead.

Bounding down three flights of stairs, she realized what she'd said. She had promised to come back.

· ·

Her dad called that night at eight-thirty and again in the morning. "We'll be home by dark," he promised, even after Lorrie had insisted she was fine.

And she was, too. A day of dozing by the pool had been wonderful for her aching muscles, and the visit to Molly had left her feeling more peaceful than she'd felt all week.

She was back in her tiny suit and leafing through the Sunday paper when the date caught her eye. "Oh my God!" she cried out loud. It was the deadline Molly had given her for the assignments. With Molly going into the hospital, Lorrie had completely forgotten.

She closed the comics and left them neatly for her father. *What difference does it make that the work was due today?* she asked herself. Molly wouldn't know she was unprepared.

But Lorrie couldn't let it go. She'd never missed a deadline in her life. Even when she was home sick, she'd tried to get her schoolwork in on time. It was a thing with her. Her mother used to tease her about it: "You're so much like your dad," she'd say.

Lorrie gave up trying to pretend that it didn't matter. She knew it was silly, but if her assignment was due today, she was going to have it ready.

She dressed and got to work. The first thing she did was gather up her prints. There were so many! She knew her box of printing paper was just about empty, but, still, she was surprised when she looked down at the tall stack. She'd taken a lot of pictures this summer, more than she had during two semesters with the school paper.

Before she sorted through the pictures, she reread the assignment, written in Molly's old-fashioned script. There were four different sections, and Lorrie was pretty sure she had each one: a distinctive shape, a texture, a story, and an emotion.

Taking her time, she went through the prints, all of them, not just the ones she had shot for the assignment, sorting them into piles on the dining-room table, where she had come to work. First she separated out the pictures she knew she wouldn't use, the ones of Sarah and her sister, of her dad and Elaine, of Thomas with Bullet. She lingered over those of Molly in the garden and then put these to the side. She wanted to go back into the darkroom and work some more on them. But for now, the goal was to get this four-part assignment in order.

It took a long time, selecting and discarding, but at last she was done. Four neat rows lay before her on the glossy wood. It was time for a break.

After lunch, she returned to the table, determined to look as objectively as possible at the pictures she'd spent weeks shooting.

Her heart sank. There was something wrong in each and every shot, she realized sadly. A poor exposure here, a bad angle there. It was too late to do anything about it. The assignment was due today.

"Good thing Molly can't see this," she said. But as soon as the words were out of her mouth, she knew they weren't true. It wasn't good that Molly couldn't see these pictures. Not good at all.

She wanted Molly back.

● ●

Yesterday's hospital visit had broken the ice, and Lorrie stayed a long time today. She went down and bought a magazine from the gift shop and read it from cover to cover, making herself comfortable in the chair by Molly's window. Then she turned on the TV and watched an old movie. Still Molly slept. The nurses came and went. The floor was quiet except for the low murmur of families visiting and the occasional burst of laughter down in the lounge.

When she left the hospital hours later, Lorrie wasn't quite ready to go home. The air-conditioning made Molly's room chilly, and Lorrie was stiff from sitting all afternoon. Back on her bike, she strapped on her helmet and set off on a long ride through Bethesda, over to Silver Spring, and back through the park, finally ending up at the riding stables. Lorrie waved a hand at Shane, who was giving a lesson in the ring, and went to find Niki.

Her horse was in her stall, as usual. "Have you missed me?" Lorrie said to the old white mare. She picked up the brush and ran it over the slumped back. "I missed you," she murmured in Niki's ear. "It's just you and me. Everybody else is gone, aren't they?" Thomas was on vacation for another week, and Sarah until right before school started. Lorrie thought about Molly, who was sleeping her days away in the hospital. How long would it be before someone started talking about moving Molly to a nursing home? Lorrie concentrated on pulling tangles from Niki's mane. She didn't even want to think of that.

twenty-two

Her parents were home, Lorrie observed, pedaling into the driveway. There on the front porch was a new potted plant, probably something they'd picked up at some roadside stand. Her weekend alone was over.

"You're back early," she said when she found them by the pool. They'd been back for some time. The newspaper had been read, and there were empty plates beside their chairs.

Her dad jumped up to give her a big hug. Over her shoulder, he said, "Yes, I've got a big meeting tomorrow morning, and I have a few more things to do to prepare." His hair was still wet from swimming, and he smelled of chlorine. He pulled back, holding on to both her hands. "Your pictures, Lorrie," he said, smiling broadly, "they are wonderful. Really quite good. I am truly impressed."

Elaine was nodding in agreement.

It was all Lorrie could do not to hit herself in the head. How stupid of her! They probably thought that she'd deliberately left her work out on display for them to see.

But she was sure when she left that she'd be back before they returned.

"Those shots of the Vietnam Veterans Memorial are splendid," he raved. "Thanks so much for leaving them out for us."

Lorrie didn't want to talk about her work. The pictures were okay, but not wonderful. Not splendid. Not even close to what Molly could do. "You'll have to tell me about your trip. I'm going to change out of these clothes. I'm hot and dirty from my ride," she said, squirming out of her father's grasp and heading toward the sliding door.

Elaine caught up with her. "Lorrie, if you've got a second," she said, "I bought you a little something."

Inside, she handed Lorrie a bag with a picture of mountains on the front of it. "I saw it and thought of you."

It was a book of photographs from Appalachia.

"A couple of the pictures in there reminded me of one of the prints I saw in your darkroom last week." She shrugged. "Thought there were some neat techniques you might like to see."

Lorrie flipped through the book. The pictures were black-and-whites from the turn of the century, mostly of families living in the mountains. "Thank you," she said, stopping at a picture that reminded her of the old house Thomas had shown her by the creek. She liked the way the photographer had used early-morning streams of light to give the shot the focal point her own pictures were missing. She'd have to try that. "Thanks so much. I love it," she repeated, giving her stepmom a quick kiss on the cheek.

Elaine tossed ice cubes into two plastic glasses. "Can I make you a drink?"

"Please."

"You enjoyed the weekend?"

"It was fun." Later, she'd tell her about her visits with Molly. The days spent working alone with Elaine gave them plenty of time to talk. In the last couple of weeks, they'd learned a lot about each other. Sometimes, when Elaine was talking about something that had happened to her in college or in a special case in court, Lorrie wondered how things would have been between them if not for the work they shared.

"I enjoyed your pictures, too," Elaine said, handing Lorrie a glass of iced tea. She grabbed two more glasses in one hand and pulled the sliding door open with the other. "I'm sorry if you didn't mean for us to see them."

Lorrie reached over to help with the door. "It's okay. I just wish they were better," she admitted.

"Yeah?"

"Yeah," Lorrie said, and let it go at that.

In the dining room, she stood over her work, trying to see what her father and Elaine had seen. Her dad had seemed genuinely impressed, and he was, after all, a curator at a museum. He worked with photography on every exhibit. Was there really something good here?

Trying to keep an open mind, she picked up each print. Her work was better, she had to admit, than what she'd been shooting at the beginning of the summer, but still. . . .

The longer she stood there, the clearer her mistakes became. The shots on shapes and textures were confusing, most of them too cluttered with other stuff. And the story assignment with the little girl was cute, but what, really, was compelling about a group of kids taking a riding lesson? Where was the message there? It wasn't like Molly's Vietnam-soldier shots, where the pictures said something.

The only shots that were at all good were the few she'd printed from the Vietnam Memorial, but now Lorrie could see that *these* were the shots that told a story.

By the time she was through critiquing her own work, all her neat rows were gone. The work of the morning was totally undone.

She left the pictures scattered across the tabletop. Maybe her father and Elaine thought the pictures were good, and maybe even Molly would, too. But Lorrie didn't like them.

Her mind was made up. She was going to shoot the entire assignment again.

....

Putting paint on the walls was the payback for all the weeks of prep work. "Molly is going to love this," Lorrie said several times a day, whenever she was admiring a just-painted floorboard, or the crown molding along the top of a room, or the changing colors of a wall as the sunlight hit it.

The work went quickly. With help from the professional painter Elaine had hired, the three of them were going to be finished with the entire first floor by the end of the week. A small crew was on the outside, too, painting the white brick and black shutters.

Into these busy workdays, Lorrie fit as much picture-taking as she could. It was different now. She didn't think about Molly's response to the shot. Instead, she thought about what *she* wanted to see, and then worked to get it. For the first time, ever, she was shooting for herself.

She began with shapes and played with her camera, switching lenses, turning it at an angle, slowing down the shutter speed. Then she went back to the assignment on texture, choosing to work in one of her favorite places, the woods. She was trying to capture sunlight on leaves and tree trunks, but she wouldn't know how successful these new pictures were until she developed the film. And that was the part she was balking at. She still hadn't returned to the darkroom.

Each day, too, she visited Molly. Tired of magazines and television, she started bringing in her books on photography. Some of the books were technical, but she had one that contained essays about art. Lorrie, thinking Molly might just like to hear the sounds of a human voice, read these out loud. Sometimes she would forget that her friend was asleep and she'd stop to ask a question or to catch Molly's expression when something seemed particularly interesting, but Molly's face was always the same—peaceful and still. Elaine had told her the doctors saw signs that Molly was coming out of the coma, but Lorrie was tired of waiting.

. . . .

Lorrie finally reached the point where she couldn't avoid the darkroom any longer. The top of her dresser was covered with black plastic containers of shot film. If she didn't start developing, she would never catch up.

On Saturday morning, she let herself into Molly's house and stood in the foyer for a long time. Yesterday they'd hung pictures back on the walls and put new blinds on the windows. The curtains, which had been cleaned, were back up as well. Lorrie couldn't wait for Molly to see it.

Postponing her trip down to the darkroom, she retreated to the backyard. She couldn't bear to sit on the bench without Molly, so she pulled weeds instead. Then she mowed the lawn. "Queen of the delay tactics," she murmured to herself when she was done.

At last it was time. She slung her backpack full of canisters of film over her shoulder and descended the wooden stairs.

The room was as she had left it that horrible night weeks ago. Molly's chair was turned over on the floor. The paper wrappers from the IV needles lay scattered where the emergency workers had dropped them. Lorrie moaned when she saw Molly's green sweater in a heap against the wall.

She picked it up and hugged it to her chest. She wished Molly were here to call her "missy" or to yell at her to close the front door because the "blooming air-conditioning" was on.

Numbly, Lorrie cleaned up, putting Molly's chair back upstairs and taking out the trash. Then she wiped down all the countertops and the machines and refilled her trays with chemicals and water.

She pulled out her film rolls and lined them up on the counter. She had enough work to keep her busy for the next three days. With the odor of the chemicals back in the air and everything set up and ready to go, Lorrie felt the old excitement return.

She may have been afraid to step back into the darkroom, but now that she was here, she was in the mood for something different. She had read lots of books in the last few weeks, and she wanted to play with some new printing techniques, especially on the shapes assignment.

Yesterday she'd double-exposed a roll on purpose, just to see how this worked. And after she'd read about combining negatives on the same print, she knew she'd have to try that. By the end of the day, she was using scissors and glue, cutting and pasting to create bold, artsy collages.

She smiled as she snipped away. What would Molly have to say about today's experimenting? Did she ever step outside of photojournalism and just have fun? Lorrie would have to ask her.

....

The next day, she returned to complete the assignments. The texture section was now more about light, but she didn't care. She liked how the shots of the dappled leaves on the floor of the woods had turned out, especially on this new matte print-paper she was using.

Lorrie didn't see how she could have missed that the story assignment was in the Vietnam Memorial shots. The faces of the people, their body language, the gifts they left behind—it was all right there. She went back to the film and chose different frames to print this time.

She decided to send a couple to Ms. Hanson, her history teacher, along with the rubbing. Then she printed a few for Thomas, who'd given her the idea to go.

Pleased with her new work in the darkroom, she once again returned to the dining-room table at home. Elaine and her dad were in the kitchen, preparing pasta salads for a couple of nights' worth of dinners, as they sometimes did on Sunday evenings. Lorrie worked for a while, arranging and discarding and sometimes taking her scissors to crop a print, so that she would know what to do when she returned to the darkroom to try it again.

In the end, she was left with three full columns of work. The fourth assignment, the one on emotion, was still missing.

Lorrie stared at the empty space on the table where the final assignment should have gone. Why was this one so hard?

When Elaine stuck her head in the doorway, Lorrie waved her in.

Elaine looked down at the columns of pictures. "I like these. What are you doing? Is this another assignment, a different one from last week?"

"Same one."

"I thought you were finished."

Lorrie shrugged. "I'm just fooling around with it a little more." She pointed to the empty space where the fourth assignment should have been. "I'm missing one."

"But you had four before."

"I know." Lorrie explained how she had rearranged the rows. Then she told Elaine about all the pictures she'd taken in the past week, trying to capture an emotion. She spread out her fingers and counted off the places she'd been to in her free time. "I went to the playground and got kids on the sliding board. I stood on the traffic island at rush hour and shot pictures of angry drivers. I even hung around that group of dog walkers over at the park to get pictures of them drooling over their dogs the way they do." She thought of the pictures at Molly's that she and Elaine had just rehung. Molly had emotion in every shot, and Lorrie would bet that she didn't have to go out searching for it. "Nothing I'm shooting works. Nothing even comes close."

Elaine shrugged her shoulders. "I don't know what to tell you. I guess you'll know it when you've got it."

"I guess. . . ." Lorrie started to gather up her prints.

"Leave them out," insisted Elaine. "We like looking at your work."

. . . .

Molly was stirring more, showing signs of moving into a lighter sleep, and the doctors were very encouraged. Lorrie was pleased but strangely impatient, too. Sometimes she would stare at Molly's peaceful face, willing her to wake up and talk to her. Lorrie's favorite nurse came into the room one day and caught her pleading with Molly, "Please, Molly, just open your eyes for a minute."

Lorrie felt embarrassed, but the nurse just smiled and said, "She'll come around in her own time, honey." She reached for Molly's arm to take her blood pressure. "Her brain is healing itself. She'll wake up when she's ready. It shouldn't be much longer."

Back at Molly's, Elaine and Lorrie started work upstairs. This was complicated, because the rooms were filled with furniture and personal stuff, and they had to design an elaborate system of labeling so they could get everything back to where it had been. Finally, Lorrie hit on the idea of labeling things in place and then taking pictures. That done, they shifted things from room to room as they painted one area at a time.

Washington in August was boring, Lorrie decided. She was tired of summer vacation, and she was tired of going to Molly's house. She wished Thomas and Sarah were home. They'd both sent her postcards last week. Lorrie was beginning to feel like she was the only person who was stuck home all summer.

Every four or five days, she called her mom. Her mother had a job in an organic restaurant. She was excited about the people she was working with, and Lorrie was happy for her, but each day she felt a little more sorry for herself.

Then, one day, she'd had enough. She couldn't bear the thought of going to Molly's.

"My wrist hurts," she whined to Elaine.

Elaine left her in bed. At the end of the day, when Elaine came home and complained that Lorrie had left her dirty dishes in the sink and trash by the pool, Lorrie stormed out of the house.

On foot for a change, there weren't a lot of places Lorrie felt like going. She decided to go and see Molly. Still in a foul mood, she took the elevator instead of the stairs, like she usually did. In her grumpiness, she got off on the wrong floor.

She was out of the elevator and well into the corridor before she realized her mistake. It was the cheery-faced clown picture on the wall that tipped her off. Lorrie scowled at it and was turning to leave when she caught sight of the child at the end of the long hallway.

The boy was standing in a wide beam of sunlight that streamed through the unshaded window. He was dressed in light-colored pajamas, and his hair was a white-blond. But what really gave him a ghostly image was his skin. It was a pale, pale pink, far too light to have seen much summer sun.

She tried to guess his age. Ten, she supposed. She took a few steps closer. He had tubes in his arm and a tall silver IV pole beside him. He gestured for her to come nearer.

All along the corridor were rooms full of kids in beds with parents sitting beside them. Stuffed animals lined the windowsills, and colorful balloons were tied to chairs. When Lorrie reached the boy, she decided that he was a lot older than ten.

"Hi," he said. His voice was thin and raspy, and Lorrie got a quick impression that tubes might have made it raw.

"I'm lost," she began to explain, a little nervously. "I mean, I'm on the wrong floor. I came to visit a friend and got off the elevator too soon."

With a directness that surprised her, he asked, "What's wrong with your friend?"

"She's old," Lorrie responded without thinking. "I mean, she's asleep. A stroke, if you know what that is. She collapsed a few weeks ago, and now she's just asleep. The doctors are optimistic," she concluded, speaking hospital-talk.

Down the hall, a small child started to cry, and they both listened to the low, soothing sounds of a father trying to comfort him.

The boy pushed his IV stand forward. "I'm going back to my room." He was heading in the direction of the stairs, so Lorrie fell into step beside him. "Usually I'm down at Children's," he said, referring to the pediatric hospital downtown, "but this way my parents can stop in during the day, right from work."

"That's good," Lorrie said, remembering how her mom had stayed with her every minute when she'd had her tonsils taken out.

"This is a long walk for me. Usually I just sit in bed and read or watch TV, but today I was bored, bored with everything."

"Me, too," Lorrie admitted, and then immediately felt guilty because she wasn't the one sick and in the hospital.

"Do you drive yet?"

"No, I'm only fifteen."

"I'm fourteen. But people think I'm younger because I'm small. And sick. Leukemia. Cancer of the blood." He looked at her to see if she needed to hear more.

She didn't. They were at his door. He leaned up against the frame and stopped. He didn't want to go back to bed, Lorrie guessed. She nodded toward the bed. "Go on, lie down. I'll stay for a couple of minutes. We can be bored together."

She ended up telling him all about Molly and the dark-room and the assignment she was still trying to shoot.

His eyes brightened. "That sounds like fun. I like taking pictures, too."

They talked about the cameras they owned and the ones they dreamed of having. He was into the newest digital stuff. Lorrie liked hearing about it.

When his eyes started to droop, Lorrie stood up to go. "Molly says a good photographer never goes anywhere without a camera, and here I am without mine."

"Yeah, me, too. There's good shots here, you know," he said. "Come back with your camera. I'll introduce you to some kids."

Lorrie thought about it. *Why not?* she figured. "I'll come back tomorrow. Early, because I have to work," she added, leaving him to the nurse who entered the room.

She had gone all the way up to Molly's room before she realized that she'd never asked his name.

twenty-three

His name, she discovered, was Michael. Maybe it was his frailty that led Lorrie to misjudge him, but she never dreamed Michael would teach her so much.

His eyes were half shut when she came into the room the next morning, but when he saw the camera, he perked up. Taking it from her, he quickly checked out all the settings and then led the way to the first young patient.

In each room, he addressed the child by name. "I'm taking pictures. Is that okay?" he'd ask. No one turned him down.

The children loved the camera—or at least they did when Michael was behind it. "Take a picture of me doing this," they would demand, making silly faces or pretending to rip out their IVs. "Get a picture of my mom." Or "Get a picture of my toys."

It wasn't all silliness, either. Michael would get them to talk about what they were scared of and what they hated most. While the kids described things like throwing up alone or having to go to the bathroom with someone watching you or that scared feeling they got when they woke up after surgery, Michael hit the shutter again and again, listening intently all the while.

Lorrie stayed by Michael's side until he was too tired to lift the camera. Then she helped him back to his room.

"I'll be back tomorrow with prints," she promised.

He waved but didn't bother to open his eyes as she tip-toed out.

....

She worked until late that night and again the next morning, making prints for Michael and the kids. Michael's pictures had her assignment on emotion nailed. The wide smiles, the wet eyes on somber faces, the laughter of a little girl covered in bandages from head to toe—a single dominant emotion in every single shot.

How had he done it? Lorrie had been right by his side, and she still didn't know.

....

Lorrie took the hospital stairs two at a time. She couldn't wait to show Michael what he'd done. She had his name on her lips when she entered the room. The sound died when she saw that the bed was stripped and empty.

She was standing, dazed, when a nurse came in with sheets for the bed.

"Looking for Michael?" she asked kindly.

"I've got something for him," Lorrie said, holding up the envelope.

"Oh, you must be his friend with the camera. He left his address at the nurses' station. And his phone number. He wants you to call him." She looked over expectantly, waiting for Lorrie's response.

"I will," she promised.

The nurse straightened the bottom sheet.

Lorrie lingered in the doorway. "So will he be okay?"

The nurse met her gaze. "That's what we are all hoping. He's a strong boy. He's getting the best care."

That was enough for Lorrie. She didn't want to know any more. She visited each child from the day before and distributed the pictures. Michael had told them all that she'd be back.

She was leaving the ward when she heard the faint noise of babies crying. She cocked her head and listened. It was the distinctive sound of newborns, and it was coming through the double doors at the other end of the hall.

"Wow," Lorrie exclaimed when she discovered the rows of babies in the hospital nursery. Each lay in its own little plastic bassinet, wrapped in a white flannel blanket. "You guys are so adorable," she murmured, wishing Sarah could see this, too.

She stood there for a while, just staring at the tiny things. A couple of times she lifted up the camera and framed a shot, but the glare from the glass interfered.

Other people joined her. Visiting hours must have started, because the room was full of families—grandparents and fathers and little kids who were being lifted and shown their new brother or sister. It was a noisy, happy crowd.

"Would you look at that head of hair?" asked the woman standing next to Lorrie. Her voice was warm and friendly. Lorrie smiled at the black-haired baby being held by the doctor who was examining him.

Then a white-haired man on her left nudged Lorrie and pointed to his grandchild. "He's the spitting image of his father. I want you to tell me if you don't agree." He grabbed her sleeve and pulled her back a few steps until she was face-to-face with a plump man in a blue sports jacket who looked like he hadn't stopped smiling all day.

Lorrie made a show of looking at the younger man's face and back to the infant several times before she nodded her head in agreement. The man grinned even wider, if that was possible.

"Which one is yours?" the white-haired man asked.

Lorrie suddenly realized what he must think with her standing here for so long. "Oh, no, I just heard the babies crying and came to look."

"Well, I'm glad you did," said the beaming grandfather, as if she'd dropped by his own home. He glanced at her camera. "That camera made me think one of them was yours."

"Oh, no. I'm taking some lessons, actually, and I . . ." Then it came to her. If she couldn't capture emotion in this place, she might as well give up.

The old man quickly agreed to help her with her assignment. He even requested that "his baby" be brought out for some family shots. It wasn't exactly what Lorrie was planning on, but how could she object?

She had a cooperative group. Too cooperative, it turned out. These pictures were as staged as any she'd taken. The grandfather gave her his business card, and she promised to mail him the prints. Her work was all over town, it seemed.

I'm never going to get this assignment, she was thinking to herself, when she saw the woman standing alone at the back of the crowd.

She wore a bathrobe like the other mothers, and her stomach was big and puffy out front as if she were still pregnant, but that's where the similarities ended.

Lorrie stepped away from the group and slipped a longer lens onto her camera without even looking down at her hands. She'd need more light at this distance, but it might work if she kept her shutter open longer. She looked around her for something to lean on, to hold her still while she took the shot.

The woman stared off at some middle distance. Her eyes were filled with a deep sadness that no one in the room was aware of, no one but Lorrie.

A fair-haired baby was being held up to the window. Lorrie found the angle where the glare on the glass was gone. She focused on the baby's sleeping face and the hand of the grandmother pressed up against the glass.

Lorrie smiled behind her camera and widened the shot. She liked the composition: the swaddled babies on one side, the happy crowd in the middle, and on the other side, behind the group, the lone woman with the sad face. Lorrie watched her through the camera's lens. She took in the woman's slumped posture, her huddled shoulders, the way her hands, down deep into her robe pockets, seemed to be holding her up.

Lorrie wanted the picture—and it would be so easy to hit the shutter and have it—but it wouldn't be fair. She'd done that at the Vietnam Memorial with a long lens, and it felt like cheating, taking those secret shots.

She lowered the camera. What she was seeing was grief. That numb feeling you get when you can't even cry and your body just seems to take up space. This woman's baby was not here in the nursery with all the other babies. This woman's baby had died.

Lorrie shut her eyes. The image of the woman stayed with her. The way the image of the soldier in the foxhole stayed. It was the kind of shot that would.

When she opened her eyes, the woman was looking at her. Lorrie didn't look away. A moment passed, and then another. She felt her body go still. Without knowing how or why, Lorrie's own body took on the woman's stance.

She felt the woman's pain come to her in waves.

It was familiar. Lorrie had felt it when her grandmother died, when her parents announced their divorce, when Molly collapsed in the darkroom. She had felt loss in other, lesser ways, too, like when Sarah spent all her time with her boyfriend and when Lorrie's mother left for California to start a life of her own.

A sudden burst of laughter momentarily diverted the woman's gaze. When she looked back, she glanced down at the camera. Lorrie lifted it and with a questioning tilt of her head asked silently for permission.

The woman gave the smallest of nods. It was okay. Lorrie was free to take the shot.

Slowly, Lorrie lifted the camera, keeping her eyes on the woman's face. The woman's expression had not changed: She was not going to let the camera interfere with her grief and her unspoken need to communicate it.

• • • • • • • • • • • • • • • • • • • •

The grandfather shots were fun to print, and Lorrie couldn't wait to mail them off. But the shot of the grieving woman was a different story. She loved it the instant she saw the negative. It was everything she'd intended it to be—the angles, the light, the woman's expression. At last, Lorrie had a shot she was completely pleased with.

She printed a copy and tucked it away. She wanted Molly to see it before anyone else did.

• • • • • • • • • • • • • • • • • • • •

Three days later, Molly woke up. Lorrie was sitting in the room leafing through a book on digital photography when

Molly suddenly yanked her arm away from the nurse taking her blood pressure.

"What do you think you're doing?" she demanded.

Lorrie slammed the book shut and jumped up. "Molly?"

"You don't have to shout! I'm not hard of hearing, you know."

"Molly!" Lorrie couldn't believe it. She hadn't changed at all. Lorrie fell on top of her. "Molly, you're awake, you're awake!" she said again and again, until the nurse had to pull her off.

"Don't be making such a fuss," Molly said, trying, unsuccessfully, to sound gruff.

Lorrie kissed her cheek and fell back into her chair. "We've been waiting and waiting. For weeks! You've been asleep for weeks!"

The nurse reached over to touch Lorrie's arm, to settle her down, but Molly didn't need her to. "You'll have to wait just a little longer," she said, and shut her eyes again.

Lorrie panicked. "Molly?"

The nurse patted Lorrie's shoulder. "It's okay, dear. She's still going to be sleeping quite a bit."

Molly briefly opened her eyes again, gave Lorrie a small smile, and was asleep once more.

Lorrie waited around a couple more hours before Molly woke up again and managed, with her help, to take a sip of water.

....

Over the next week, Molly was awake a little bit longer each day, but when Lorrie stepped off the elevator one morning and heard cursing, she knew her friend was really getting better. "Dang it all. I don't like milk. I've hated it my whole life, and I darn well don't plan to start drinking it now." Lorrie smiled when she heard the hissing sound Molly always made when she was mad.

••••••••••••••••••••

"She's driving the nurses crazy. I think they're going to get her out of there as soon as they possibly can," Lorrie told Thomas. He was back at last, and they were talking on the phone. When he'd called, Lorrie hadn't even known who he was. And then, when she recognized his voice, she couldn't believe he had called just to talk—and not about lessons at the stables, either. They chatted like old friends, catching up on what they'd been doing since they last saw each other, and made plans to get together on Sunday at their usual time.

Her reunion with Sarah was more emotional. Sarah had finally checked her e-mail, and when Lorrie picked up the phone, all she heard was screaming. "Why didn't you call me!" It took her a while to realize that Sarah was referring to the kiss. Lorrie had completely forgotten that she'd written about it.

"It was no big deal," she said, trying to sound convincing.

"I'm coming over." And then, just like old times, Sarah stayed for dinner and slept over and hung around late the next morning, too. Catching up with Sarah didn't take fifteen minutes.

••••••••••••••••••••

Every day, Molly got stronger. She complained bitterly about all the exercises they were forcing her to do in physical therapy, though Lorrie knew it was good for her. There was talk of a nursing home, but Molly would have nothing to do with that idea.

"Hell or high water," she insisted, "I'm coming home."

The other decision Molly made concerned the furniture in the house. Elaine and Lorrie had put everything back in place after they'd painted, but Molly had surprised them with a request that they go ahead and empty the house of all the things she had agreed to let go of earlier in the summer.

Elaine didn't want to rush this stage, so she put everything in a high-security storage unit until she could talk it over with Molly one more time. After she was sure that all decisions were final, she would release the furniture to the auction house and the various museum collections.

Lorrie had thought the house looked great with the new paint, but without all the furniture, it was completely transformed. The chunky end tables and ugly sofa were gone from the living room. The dining room was spacious and airy with the dark dining set gone and the smaller table and chairs set up in its place. The first-floor study was now a bedroom, so that Molly wouldn't have to climb the steps. Elaine put handrails into both bathrooms and took up all the throw rugs that might cause Molly to trip. No one dared to say the word "wheelchair" around Molly, but what Elaine and Lorrie were doing was making the house accessible.

twenty-four

Finally, it was the day of Molly's homecoming. Lorrie nervously paced the house, pulling up the blinds and then putting them back down, straightening and restraightening the framed prints on the walls. "Do you think she'll like it?" she asked. She knew she was driving Elaine crazy, but she couldn't help herself.

Elaine stood with her keys in her hand. She was going to check Molly out of the hospital while Lorrie waited here. "She'll let us know. She always does."

After Elaine drove off, Lorrie had an inspiration. She went to the backyard and picked bunches of flowers. A surprising number had taken root among the weeds and bloomed still, year after year. She placed them on the dining-room table, beside Molly's bed, and on the mantel in the living room.

At last she heard Elaine's car in the driveway. Lorrie grabbed her camera and ran to the front window.

Molly was home.

Lorrie got a lump in her throat when she saw her friend.

Assisted by a walker, Molly looked more fragile than ever before. Slowly, so very slowly, and with Elaine's help, Molly took small steps up the pathway. Halfway along, she stopped and looked up at her house. The facade and shutters had been painted in her absence, the first of many changes that awaited her. Her smile brought tears to Lorrie's eyes.

Then Molly saw Lorrie at the window and raised a hand in greeting. Lorrie waved back and ran out the front door. "Molly," she cried. "Welcome home!" She'd told Molly that she was going to take pictures at the homecoming, and now she did, catching Molly's familiar scowl at having to maneuver the walker, and her smile when she stepped into the foyer and shut the door behind her.

The old photographer stood there in the wide center

hall for a long time, her head turning this way and that as she took in the new look of her home.

Over her head, Lorrie exchanged worried glances with Elaine. Would Molly like it? Would it be too much?

Finally, Molly pushed her walker forward, making her way farther into the house. "Very nice," she pronounced, in that no-nonsense way of hers. "It's just as I envisioned it." She stepped into the living room and stopped short at the sight of the mantelpiece. Lorrie had spent three days stripping it down to the bare wood and then repainting it. "Except for this," said Molly, running her finger over the intricate grape-leaf border that Lorrie had uncovered. "This is a wonderful surprise." Her glance went to the bouquet of black-eyed Susans. "Oh, and flowers from Albert's garden."

Elaine shot Lorrie a questioning glance. Elaine knew little about the backyard garden and nothing at all about Albert Blake.

Molly was clearly exhausted. Elaine tried to persuade her to lie down, but Molly had other plans. "I have an announcement to make," she said, starting off in the direction of the kitchen. "And I'd like some tea."

Lorrie hurried ahead of them and had it on the table as Molly entered the room.

Elaine pulled out her pencil and clipboard.

"Put that away," directed Molly. "What I have to say is simple enough." Her hand shook as she returned her teacup to the saucer. Then she spied the old green sweater, which Lorrie had washed and mended and left out for her. With Lorrie's help, she put it on.

"Now, where were we?" Molly asked.

"You have something to tell us, I believe," said Elaine.

"Yes. I had a lot of time to think while I was in that hospital, and I've made a few decisions."

Elaine and Lorrie waited expectantly.

"First and foremost," Molly began, "I am not selling this house." She waved her hand at Elaine, who opened her mouth to protest. "Second, I'm not leaving here to go live anywhere else. You can pull my name from that waiting list, Elaine."

"But, Molly—"

Molly ignored her. "Now, another thing," she continued. "I plan on leaving all my papers to that college professor over at the journalism school at Maryland, but I've got a few stipulations." She looked straight at Lorrie and then back to Elaine.

Lorrie squirmed in her seat. Something else was coming. Something that involved her.

Molly's eyes were alert and focused, her teacup steady in her hand. She directed her gaze at Elaine. "A while back, you mentioned to me that Lorrie here might be the one to talk to me about my life." She chuckled. "Well, we certainly have already talked about my life, haven't we, dear?" she asked, smiling at Lorrie.

Lorrie just nodded.

"I don't know if you were serious about this, Elaine, but I am. I've thought about it and thought about it, and I think this young lady is a fine listener. And she asks a lot of questions, too. I've told her a good deal about my life already, and I find that I have some more to say. So—you can let that Dunn woman know that if Lorrie would like to conduct the interview then I'm ready to get started on that."

Lorrie sat very still.

"I don't even know if this is something that interests you, Lorrie," Molly added. "I got to thinking when you asked me about those pictures of the soldier and about Albert here," she said, gesturing to the back door. "I got to thinking that I wanted to tell some of these stories, that there are things I would like to say. And I can't write them down, and I don't feel like talking to a bunch of strangers."

"I've been writing them down," Lorrie said without thinking.

Elaine's and Molly's eyes were instantly on her.

"You've been writing what down?" demanded Molly.

"Stories. I have a file in my computer. 'The Stories of Molly Price,'" Lorrie said. "Just parts of stories, really, things you've said to me."

"Well, I'll be," Molly said.

"But if we taped them, like Natalie Dunn wants to, it would be better," Lorrie told her. "We'd have the sound of your voice, and all the details, not just the ones that I tried to remember later at my computer."

"That's right," agreed Elaine. "There's so much to tell,

Molly. You've been a part of so many important events in this country. People want to know what it was like to be there."

Lorrie felt herself getting excited. But there was something she needed to ask.

"Molly," she began, "if you want to give an interview, why give it to me? There are scholars who are much more qualified."

Molly was quiet for a long moment. Lorrie was starting to think she'd forgotten the question when she looked at Lorrie and began to speak.

"I want you to do it because I think you'd do a good job. I think you are young and curious and smart. And you will prepare yourself like a lawyer going before the Supreme Court, like an astronaut preparing for space. You will put your heart into this, and when you do, you will learn about photography and history and people, not just about me. You will learn this because you are thorough, and you will study hard before you ask a single question." She cocked her head. "Am I right?"

Lorrie didn't have to think long. She had already thought of it herself. She'd done an interview or two for the school paper. She knew the value of preparation. "Yes, Molly, you're right."

Molly turned to Elaine. "Your daughter here is a talented young woman and has the makings of a fine photographer, even though she is a little hard on herself and expects to learn in a day something that may take years. I look forward to this project. You tell that Natalie Dunn not to call me. She will work directly with the two of you."

Molly shuffled in her seat as if she were about to get up. "Wait, there's one more thing," she said. "I'm doling out money all over the place, aren't I, Elaine?"

"Um, yes, Molly, you are setting up some generous scholarships—" she began.

"That's correct. And I'd like Lorrie here to benefit as well."

Lorrie didn't quite understand. Was Molly talking about college? Elaine looked puzzled, too.

"I'm talking about these interviews. I want her to have a contract. A good one."

Lorrie hadn't even considered this.

"All right. We'll have to talk more about this," agreed Elaine.

Molly took a sip of her tea. "They didn't have good tea in the hospital," she said. "The water was never hot enough."

A moment of silence fell as they took it all in: Molly's homecoming, her announcement about staying, her offer to work with Lorrie and Natalie Dunn.

Then Molly pushed back her saucer and, with the help of her walker, stood up and faced them. "We'll talk again tomorrow. I just wanted to get a few things settled and to let this frightened-looking young lady here, who is probably going to get herself worked into a lather over this, know that I have confidence in her. She is going to do great things."

Elaine grinned at Lorrie, who was feeling embarrassed to be the subject of all this attention.

"Oh, there's one last thing," said Molly, catching Elaine's eye and then Lorrie's.

What on earth could that be? thought Lorrie.

Molly hesitated for a long time and then cleared her throat and began to speak. "I just want to thank you both—for being here with me now, and for taking care of me while I was at the hospital." Her voice broke but, she went on. "It means a lot to me, and I want you both to know how much I appreciate it."

Lorrie and Elaine began to cry. And then they were dabbing their eyes with their napkins.

Lorrie started to laugh first. Molly and Elaine joined her.

"My friends," Molly finally said, "I'm worn out, so you'll have to excuse me." She turned her walker around, as she'd learned in physical therapy, and headed to the door.

Elaine hopped up, but Lorrie remained at the table. She needed a moment alone. From the other room, she heard the thud of the walker and Molly muttering: "I don't like people fussing over me, so don't even think about getting me one of those blasted beepers that you talked about in the hospital, Elaine."

Lorrie listened to Molly getting settled. It was great to have her home. Later, maybe tomorrow, after Molly was rested, Lorrie wanted to show her the pictures she'd been working on. She'd put a lot of them in notebooks, and a couple of shots she'd matted and framed. She wanted Molly to see what she had learned—and what she'd been given. She was thinking of that woman in the bathrobe. Lorrie had come to believe that photography was skill and luck. And something more, something she wasn't totally sure of yet, something about trust.

....

On Sunday morning, Lorrie headed for the stables. She was suddenly feeling very shy. It had been weeks since she and Thomas had been together, and she wondered now if there had really been anything between them, or if she had just let her imagination turn a crush into something more.

Thomas's greeting at the stables ended that doubt. As

soon as she walked into the office, where he was sitting at the desk, he jumped up. "Lorrie," he said warmly. He shut the office door partway, slipping out of the line of vision of anyone who might be walking by, and reached for her hand. Quickly, he pulled her toward him and kissed her. "I'm so glad to see you," he said, then kissed her again before letting her go and kicking the door back open.

She wanted to talk to him, but not here.

"Can we ride?" she asked.

He grinned. "Are my ears deceiving me? Lorrie Taylor wants to ride!"

Out on the trail, he looked over at her. "I've never seen you look so happy. What is it? I know you're happy because Molly is back home, and I know you're glad to see me," he teased, "but there's something else. What's up?"

Lorrie laughed. She was enjoying this.

Thomas slid off his horse and reached for her. They were at their spot on the creek. "So tell me. You look like you're going to burst."

She told him about Elaine's earlier suggestion and about how she'd been stewing over it for weeks, and then she told him everything that Molly had said yesterday. "She's talking about a real interview, the kind that will be recorded and written up for the history books. And for money, too. She wants me to have a contract." When she saw that his mouth had dropped open with surprise, she giggled nervously. "One minute I think I can do it. Then I think of all the preparation I'll have to do. It can't just be stupid questions."

"Yeah? And the problem is?"

"And, well, I am just a kid."

Thomas laughed. "And you panic."

Lorrie hated the way this felt, happy one second and scared to death the next. "I don't know if I can do it."

"Of course you can," he said simply, brushing back her bangs with the fingers of his free hand.

"Of course I can?" Lorrie repeated, barely breathing.

"You're smart, right? You're good at learning stuff."

Until this summer, she'd been as sure of her ability to learn as she was of anything. But the problems she'd had with her picture-taking made her doubt herself. It had taken her the entire summer to get a single picture she was happy with. All summer to get one good shot.

Thomas laughed. "You're missing what's so exciting here."

"What?"

"The risk."

"The risk?" Lorrie said, turning the word over in her head. The birds flew in and out of the half-standing house. The horses stepped into the creek to drink. *Risk.* All her life she had *avoided* risks, playing it safe, seeking out only those things she was sure she could succeed at. But here was something for which there were no guarantees, and it was something she could not—would not—turn down.

She felt a smile form on her lips. And then a laugh bubbled up inside of her that made her shoulders shake. She felt happy, happier than she could ever remember feeling in her whole life.

"What did your dad say?" Thomas asked.

"He said that it's a wonderful—"

They completed the sentence together—"opportunity."

"I'm scared to death," Lorrie added when they were back on their horses. She didn't want anyone to think this was going to be easy for her.

"I know," Thomas said seriously. "But, personally, I think it's okay to be a little bit scared. It won't stop you from succeeding, you know."

Of course he was right. A little fear wouldn't stop her. A little fear could be overcome.

"You lead," Thomas said, pulling back to let Niki go first up the steep bank.

"She's never let me."

"Show her who's boss."

Lorrie grinned. Of course she was the boss of this little white horse. She kicked in her heels. Niki went a few feet up the path, fighting the reins, then stopped, waiting for Thomas's horse to come on ahead.

But today Lorrie was the one in charge. She leaned forward, kicking Niki into a trot and then into a canter.

The trail came up fast before them, but not too fast for Lorrie. She leaned over Niki's head, loving the smell of her horse, the warmth of this animal beneath her, the sound of the hooves hitting the dirt trail. The wind whipped her hair across her eyes, blinding her for a moment, quickening her pulse, and then blew free.

Somewhere behind was her new boyfriend, her first real boyfriend, but for now it was just Lorrie and Niki, on their own, moving swiftly along the hard path that cut through the thick green woods.